Private Correspondences

Private Correspondences

Trudy Lewis

TRIQUARTERLY BOOKS
NORTHWESTERN UNIVERSITY PRESS
Evanston, Illinois

TriQuarterly Books
Northwestern University Press
Evanston, Illinois 60208-4210

ISBN 0-8101-5033-6

Library of Congress Cataloging-in-Publication Data

Lewis, Trudy (Trudy L.)
    Private correspondences / Trudy Lewis.
        p.   cm.
    ISBN 0-8101-5033-6
    1. Teenage girls–United States–Fiction. 2. Violence–United
    States–Fiction. I. Title.
    PS3562.E978P75   1994
    813'.54–dc20   94-25843
                                                        CIP

The paper used in this publication meets the minimum requirements of the
American National Standard for Information Sciences–Permanence of Paper
for Printed Library Materials, ANSI Z39.48-1984.

For Frank, Linda, and Terry:

the better storytellers, who filled my childhood

with love and language

And for Mike Barrett, the mad poet in my life

acknowledgments

I would like to thank my teachers, editors, and fellow writers for their wise balance of enthusiasm and criticism. Alan Friedman and Lore Segal were crucial from the beginning. I am also indebted to my peers–Jeff Carney, Tony Del Valle, Beth Franken, Rob Moore, Melinda Rooney, and Steve Tomasula–who gave generously of their time while they were engaged with novels of their own.

I am grateful to Mike Barrett for his support, praise, patience, passion, imagination, and computer skills. In addition, I owe thanks to a number of friends who helped me through the trying times of doubt and discouragement. Though they did not work directly with the text, they provided much of the courage and intellectual grist that allowed me to complete the novel. They are: James Chrobak, Anita Dellaria, John Kimsey, Glynis Kinnan, Colleen Page, and Eve Wiederhold.

Private Correspondences

i

When I first got your letter, I was only fifteen. Dot and I were playing tennis in the street with our parents' wooden his-and-hers rackets, using a woozy line of tar to stand for the net. Part of the challenge was just maneuvering in the long gauze dresses our father had bought us for one of his campaign receptions, and which we insisted on wearing at every possible opportunity. We didn't really know how to play; we were only interested in shocking the neighbors, and as we batted the ball back and forth, we tried to keep the rhythm of the musical we were singing to each other as we went. Probably it was *Oliver!* that day. *Oliver!* was our favorite. We liked the part about the pickpockets, although we'd never even shoplifted ourselves—our father's career was too important for us to be taking risks like that.

Dot could pitch her voice a little lower than mine, so she took the harmony and I lit into the high notes like nobody's politics, like the sheer whine off a microphone before the speaker starts to speak. Melody is fine—I still sing it whenever I can—but it means more when you feel someone singing beneath you, slicing the song into its fifths and thirds and intervals, opening up the music.

The postman was late that Saturday, I remember. Dot went up to his jeep while he was still parked at the Greersons'.

"Wait," he said, when she started to walk away, balancing the mail on the face of her racket like a pizza. "You're more popular than that, doll." Then he came up with another stack.

We were always proud, Dot and I, that we got more mail than any of the neighbors. Our house was lopsided on our property, like a dingy yellow root growing out of the side of the hill. Our yard wasn't much better, with its cracked stone hedges matted over with wild mint and crabgrass and clover, sparser that summer because of the drought. And both our cars were regular, square-shaped Fords. But we got two handfuls of mail every day and even more now, with Daddy's election coming up in November. There were some problems with all that mail, though. For one thing, Dot and I hardly ever got any, personally. And when we did, it tended to get mixed in with the rest, then show up six months later on the floor of Daddy's Torino. That's what happened to a letter from Dot's pen pal in West Germany, and Daddy had to play her lots of games of gin rummy to make up for it.

So when we got to the top of the driveway, Dot was already fingering through for any strays. "Libby Martin," she said, and held an envelope up to our mother's ornamental lamppost, even though it was full daylight and the lamp wasn't on. "Probably from that slinky guy with the orange teeth. You know, the insect-eater."

She meant Michael Semanco, the boy I'd been in love with for almost a year. Once when he was over waiting for me to get home from a chorus concert, Dot dared him and he bit into a lightning bug, just pinched the wings closed and munched down on the yellow globe. I missed the whole thing, but Dot gave a fair imitation, crossing her big, crooked eyes, gumming up her lips, blowing on her fingers. After that, he had to eat a whole row of cheese crackers to wipe out the taste, and that's all Dot ever remembered about him, no matter how many piano awards he won, or what he looked like in a black turtleneck sweater.

"Give it here, Dottie," I said. Michael was on restriction, and we hadn't seen each other for a couple of days, and that seemed like a good enough reason for a letter. But he'd never written me before, and I wanted to read whatever he said slowly, alone, in my room.

Once I heard Dot clipping through the channels on her radio, I turned off my light and looked into the mirror. If I left the bathroom light on and turned three quarters away, mouth open, eyes to the side, I looked almost pretty. My family never mentioned it, but I varied wildly in appearance, while Dot was always lip-forward, button-down cute. But with me, well, I tried not to look into mirrors unless I was practiced up for it.

I took the letter over to my bed and pulled up the long skirt of my dress, then grabbed the honeysuckle talcum powder off the nightstand. I shook it down my thighs, over my stomach, even let a little drift onto the blond wood floor, where I rubbed it into the grain with my toes to make a soft place on the boards. Then I sat there with my dress bunched around my hips, my elbows up on the bed, beginning to read.

The letter was printed, a tall tilted print in thin black ink. It said it knew what I was after, what kind of girl I was just by watching me walk. I pushed open doors with my ass. I sucked on the opal stone of my pinkie ring. I showed up for assembly smelling the sleeve of my choir robe. I acted so innocent, pretended to act innocent, and he wasn't going to play along with me anymore.

By the time I got that far, I knew the letter wasn't from Michael. He didn't even go to my school, and, besides, he was always telling me how much I didn't know, there was stuff I couldn't even imagine. How people did it tied to beds and strapped together, standing up and sitting down and bending over underwater. What other girls said to him when he touched their breasts.

But I still thought the letter might be from one of my girlfriends who liked to talk sex at me until I stuttered, or pinch the skin of my upper arm between her extreme pink fingernails just to show certain boys how easily I bruised. Then I got to the next part of the letter, the longest part, and realized the person was no one I knew, no one I'd ever be allowed to know, or even watch on television.

What it said after that, it said he was going to rape me and cut my legs off and carve his initials on my breasts. But then he said what he was going to do again and it came out all different, with things happening in a different order and different parts of me getting cut or slashed or mangled.

It was like, I remember thinking, like you couldn't decide, and I kept on reading, because as long as I was reading I was coming alive again, getting killed another way and getting over it. And when I got to the bottom, to the name, I'd be gone for good. But not necessarily, I decided, not if I could just read fast enough. I decided it in the same way I knew I'd be all right if I ran all the way up the first twelve steps from the basement and skipped over the thirteenth, but fall and be paralyzed for life if I walked up normally. The paper made a stiff, cellophane noise, beating in my hand. My one knee sweated against the cold metal bed-frame. I was reading as fast as I could–faster–but it was still forever sitting there, like holding a note when you keep feeling the rhythm running through it, and you only want to lift your lungs and breathe.

I pushed the letter under the dresser, then fished it out again with my toes, so I wouldn't have to touch it. "X-acto," it said at the bottom. That wasn't initials. If he carved initials on me, what would he carve? Wouldn't people figure out who he was then? A shadow pain flitted under my breasts and drifted away before I could say whether it was sharp or blunted.

I got up to change my clothes, then stopped with one arm out of my dress, turned around and sat down again. Everything in my room looked different. The girl-shaped maple desk I never used, since I'd rather do homework at the kitchen table. A mysterious box tiled all over with fun-house mirrors that Dot gave me after one of her garage sale swaps. A red-and-black banner left over from Daddy's primary. I never thought my room was all that private; I didn't put up posters or slip special photographs under the rim of my mirror. The thing was, my mother made a Broadway show out of privacy, flicked her eyes over our heads and left the room when we got a phone call, bought us desks and diaries with slim metal keys. When our report cards came in the mail, she left them waiting on the kitchen counter and expected us to bring them to her. It's not that Ma'am was hypocritical; as far as I know, she didn't look or listen, either one. But it's not really privacy–nothing is–when someone makes it up and gives it to you. You know that, don't you? I guess you know it now.

Privacy didn't necessarily happen in my room. It could be anywhere, behind the drainpipe in our side yard, where there was a three-page plan for running away from home that I'd balled up inside a layer of tinfoil. Or right out in the open, in the living room, where I rubbed up against the brown satin bolster and pretended it was Michael's arm. Then there was the basement, where the furnace said "sublove" to me, and I stared into a glassy photograph of Bobby Kennedy until my reflection flexed with his.

So my room wasn't so personal to me anyway. Not until that afternoon. Because that was the change. When I looked at it again and saw all the things that meant my family, they were suddenly shocking. New and private and strange. The banner was wrinkled so the *t* didn't show, and it looked like we were named "Marin" instead. The mirrored jewelry box glinted back the light from the bathroom. These things were about my father and my mother and sister, but they were also private from them, because now there was something here they didn't know about. I was going to show them the letter all right; I never even thought of hiding it. But they wouldn't know, I couldn't tell them, what it felt like to get it.

And maybe I didn't even feel it the way I should. Maybe I was like that, like your letter said. My tongue turned rough and ripe and gummy in my mouth. I went into my bathroom, cupped my hand under the faucet, and drank in long, noisy phrases, drank until I tasted the spearmint wax of my chapstick and the clayey silt of the Roxbury Reservoir. Then when I couldn't swallow anymore, I stayed there a minute longer, letting the water run over my tongue.

Out in the hallway, Dot was playing marbles, as close to my door as she could get. They made a second-best china clatter smiting each other over the floorboards, and a duller whack when they hit against the doors or molding. I couldn't believe I hadn't heard it before; she must have been trying hard enough.

"Proposal?" she said. "I've got this idea how we can write them all down in my Bible, then add them up and split the difference. I've got two already, Peter Gottfried and Maury Durben."

Peter Gottfried was the pen pal; Maury Durben was our father's legislative assistant.

"Well, I don't have any. Besides, proposals don't count unless you're at least sixteen."

"Who says?"

"Miss Manners says. Miss Piggy says. How do I know?"

"Well, the Indians and Africans and stuff could get married as soon as they got their periods. That means Melissa Hartford could get married when she was ten and I could've married Peter last year in the seventh grade."

"Come on, Dottie. Don't be sick."

She sat back on her heels, then reached back and jiggled her ankles. "You're the one who's sick about that sleazy bug-biter. Anyway, what did he say?"

I squatted down to shoot one of her marbles. "It's not from him. It's one of those, you know, prank letters where they don't sign their name."

"What'd they say? Let me read it. I bet I know who it is."

I looked at her sitting there with her sleek, cinnamon-colored hair coiled into two wide rolls over her ears, like the princess in *Star Wars*–she figured out how to do that all by herself. And I wondered why I thought I was protecting her when it seemed like she was always growing past and protecting me instead.

"You don't know," I said. "Anyway, where's Ma'am?"

"Well, she doesn't know who wrote it."

"Forget it. No one knows who wrote it," I told her, and went around to the basement stairs.

Our mother had to be down there. If she was anyplace closer, Dot wouldn't be shooting marbles in the house. Dot wouldn't be in the house at all, but outside picking mint or pitching the softball at her favorite tree. On the way down, I stopped myself from counting by singing "Kyrie Eleison" as loud as I could. But I heard the numbers anyway, like someone was coming down behind me, saying them in my ear, adding on a number for each one I dropped. The air was cooler down there, and smelled of oil and sawdust and the fresh print of all the new campaign brochures.

Ma'am was sitting at the sewing machine in her pale blue shorts with the pleats over the pockets. They showed up her eyes, and the blue bruises scattered down her long white legs, bruises rich and deep and irregular as the hearts of geodes that Dot and I admired in our state museum. Ma'am bruised like I did, at the slightest kiss of pain, so she always had two or three bruises lingering on her legs. Daddy made jokes about buying her knee pads and shin guards to protect his political image. But she was actually serious about it, wore colored stockings to political events, and told us how people always patched together evidence in the gaudiest way they could imagine, just to get a tacky thrill. Senators and Christians, she said, have to avoid even the appearance of evil. And since Daddy was a state senator and she was a Christian, we hardly ever got away with anything.

"Ready for lunch?" she said. "Or–let me guess–you already made it, and just popped down to give me my tray."

"Ma'am," I said. She kept on working, running up the seam of Dot's new denim skirt. My senses were turning to static under the needle's dizzy drill, and the metal taste of tears behind my face made me want to sneeze.

"What is it, Lib?"

"I, I got this letter, and it doesn't say who it's from. But it's pretty scary, and I thought I should probably show it to you."

"Is it a chain letter, love?"

I slid the paper out of my pocket and gave it to her. She spread it over Dot's skirt, still holding the fabric bunched in one hand. I watched her skim down the page with her eyes skittering like skipping stones. What would happen when she got to the part about me, would she believe it? The appearance of evil, I kept thinking.

"Libby," she said. "Oh Libby, Libby, Libby love." She scraped back her chair and pulled me onto her lap, where my arms and legs and breasts really did feel cut off away from me and I wanted to tell her about the letter again then take it back and tell it over.

"Honey, there are people who'll send out letters like this. But it's a random thing. It doesn't say anything about you. It's just the person who wrote it, he's sick, disturbed. He'd say that about anybody."

I twisted a curl away from her ivory earring. "Then why'd he write to me?"

"Who knows? It takes doctors years to figure out why people do these things. And mostly, they never do find out."

"People like that, they don't really do anything–like what they say–do they?"

"Well, not usually. It's better to be careful, though. I'll get your father to call the police and see what they want us to do."

I got up and pushed some spools of thread around on the sewing table. "Don't tell Daddy. Please."

But she already had her foot back on the pedal. "Libby, I have to. He's part of the family too."

That night, Dot was going to a slumber party and Ma'am had a school board meeting at City Hall. Which left me at home alone with my father, pretending to be just alone. I closed myself in Dot's room and went through our art drawer–the good magazine covers, the greasy oil pastels, scraps and gift wrap and sequins, thick squares of colored felt we bought for no real reason and whose texture we loved more than silk or fur. But all the time I was listening to Daddy dress. He skreeked open the sliding door to the closet. He threw something heavy on the bed. He whistled a flat version of "Toreador," then turned on the bathroom faucet and turned it off again.

"Lib," he called through the door. "Do you know where your mother keeps the silver polish? I've got a problem with my cuff links here."

I pulled another stack of tablets out of the drawer. Let him wait, I thought. He ought to know how to wait.

He coughed up and down his throat. "Anybody home there, kid?"

"In the corner cabinet," I said. I reached into the back of the drawer and found something hard and slick, skinny as a finger, light as a chapstick.

"Where?"

"By the phone." I felt up the handle for the short, slanted blade. X-acto, that was it. The art knife we used to make cards and stencils with. It said its name on the side, almost the same as the one in the letter. We used it for invitations to our garage sales and announcements of our shows and the one time we sent anonymous valentines. I ran the blade over the heel of my hand, where it didn't feel like much, but left a sharp bright string of red. Like a paper cut, was all. Then I wiped the blood off on a towelette perfume sample Dot once wanted us to save.

"Lib, come on out and chat up your old man before I take off for the club."

I put the knife back in the drawer, and the perfume stung inside my cut like a thin, gaudy strip of neon. When I got to the hallway, he was standing there pulling his wingtip collar up over his chin, squinting about it, as if he felt the starch in his eyes. Then he took his glasses off and pressed his thumbs over his eyelids. He tightened up his tie.

"So what's on for tonight, kid?"

"Nothing," I said. "Maybe I'll watch videos or call Michael on the phone."

"Listen, I don't want anybody in this house. You understand?"

I didn't tell him Michael was on restriction anyway. I just said OK.

"It's enough with all those weirdos out there and the psychos on every channel of the TV. You know what some bozo tried to propose today? He wanted us to figure in a stress factor for white-collar crime. Make the sentence commutable. Concentrate on ethics programs and retraining programs. I tell you, people get ditzy at the end of these long sessions. Legislators are the only joes I know who go gaga if you tell them they have to work more than six months at a throw."

"But what about Michael?" I said.

"I'm sure he's a good kid. I just don't want you to have anyone over tonight. It's, let me show you this thing."

He led me through the hall, into his room, and over to his closet, where he went through the pockets of his suit jackets, patting each one. When he got to the blue double-breasted blazer, he came out with a little silver pistol, sleek in the half-light of the room. He pointed it down to the shoes in his closet and held his left hand over its cheek, so I couldn't see any of the moving parts.

"I didn't know you had a gun," I said.

"Somebody's great-uncle, you know how it is."

"I didn't think you liked guns. I didn't think we voted for guns."

"Don't worry, Libby. It's legal. All registered up. I just want you to know where it is in case you get scared."

He broke open the gun. "The bullets go in here. I always keep the first chamber empty, just to be sure. Now all you have to do is pull down on the trigger like that." His short, bitten fingers looked strange against the old silver stains of the gun. But he knew how to work it, I could tell he did. I felt my lungs snap closed; I couldn't stand to think he'd gotten a gun because of me, or even us, our family. Then I started to breathe again, fast, like a hiccup, when I thought maybe he would've done it anyway, and maybe that was worse.

"Here baby, you try it," he said. He stood behind me and set the gun into my hands, then left his hands over mine, helping me settle the fingers. I didn't want to do it, felt annoyed about something I couldn't remember, then recalled: my aunt's wedding, when I was seven years old. I was supposed to be the candlelighter and carry a big shepherdess's crook with a blue satin bow. Walking up the aisle, I could feel the ribbon tap my shoulder; I had to concentrate to keep from turning around. Then, at the altar, after I finished the second candle, my light went out, completely dead. But what I did, I kept on going, touching my crook to candle after candle, till I could almost see them burning there, like the weird tongues of flame in my Sunday school book. Then I saw, instead, my father coming out of the sanctuary where he'd been waiting with the groomsmen. He smiled and ducked when he got to me, he touched the wreath of flowers on my head. Out of his pocket came the tortoiseshell lighter he'd had for all my life. The people in the church made a slow, single noise, not laughing, not crying, but the wet, leaflike whimper they used to make at children when we were supposed to be especially cute. When Daddy heard that, that's when it happened. That's when he changed. He tipped his head up as he flicked the lighter. He made a little bow out of handing me back my cane. Then he did what he didn't have to, stood behind me, cradling my arms, guiding me to every candle and leading off each lighted wick with a short, jerky fillip of flame.

"Hold it just a little tighter now," he said, and clutched my fingers around the pistol. I have an octave-note fingerspan, but I still couldn't do that.

"I don't know. I don't think it's going to work."

He looked at me, and the brass-colored chips in his blue eyes got darker; the whites glistened to pink.

"This is silly, Lib. You don't like the gun, you don't have to play with it. Besides, I'd rather take you with me tonight anyway. Yeah, why shouldn't a big eater-outer like myself show off his lovely daughter at the club? So what do you say, Sly? Want to have dinner with me?"

"Yeah," I said. "That would probably be good." I slipped the gun back into his jacket, the wrong one too. But I had to get back to my room and get changed again. Because now that I was crying, and for the first time since I heard from you, all I could think of was getting away from home.

ii

So you've been to the club before; I don't have to draw the club for you. You've watched yourself walk into the lobby full of mirrors, one skinny leg edging you out past the rest of your family. You've picked at the pink and green mints with silver tongs, felt the fine leaves of soap wither onto your fingers in the gilt bathroom. You probably even dropped odd pieces of silverware into the fountain the way Dot and I used to do.

I know because I've seen you. You went one Sunday with your parents. He had a briefcase; she had a hat. They held their menus open carefully, on the flat of the hand, singers with an impressive score. Yours was spread out on the table like the Sunday comics. As you read, you rubbed at your wrist, where a normal person wears a watch. Only you had some sort of sore there. I could tell by the way your face flinched just one notch tighter every time you passed at noon. You stopped and looked around and licked your finger. You pressed it into the salt cellar. Then you went on rubbing, leading with the finger, winding up your pulse.

But that was before I knew, before I even got your letter. This night, the night with my father, there wasn't anyone around but us. They had the blue light on in the fountain and real candied squash blossoms on the dessert tray. The waiter sat us at the bay window, by the black lacquered piano that no one ever played. Maury was already there, sitting alone at a table for eight and drawing on one of the colored notecards he always carried in his suit pocket.

"Senator," he said, standing up and flicking his pen closed. "Tom."

The cards were still lying there, spread out over the heavy maroon tablecloth. Each card had basically the same picture on it—a man with an eyebrow and a half, a vampire's long nose, a witch's grin.

We both recognized him right away. But Daddy just stood there, lighting his pipe and looking out onto the golf course. "Larkin beat me here, I see."

"No fooling," Maury said. "He already ordered a drink for me. Peppermint schnapps. That's some kind of consideration, isn't it?"

I sat down and shuffled through the drawings, looking for the best one. They were almost identical, except the half eyebrow kept getting higher and shorter and more intense. Really, Larkin had two whole eyebrows: it's just that the left one was turning gray, starting from the sparse tail end of the eye and landing like a comet in the eyebrow's bushy center, where it exploded into black. Maury couldn't quite show that: I imagined him sucking on his platinum pen, shocking one of his cavities, taking out another card and trying again.

"Give me something to write with," I told Maury, who sat down and pushed his pen toward me so slowly I counted the three red hairs glazing his knuckle over the thin silver ring.

"Think you can do better, huh?"

"Maybe." I picked the cartoon I thought he drew last and attacked the blank side of the eyebrow with a band of short, slanted arrows. "There."

"OK," Maury said. "So it's an idea."

Daddy sat down, drew on his pipe again, then breathed the smoke out, very clearly, very calm. I could smell the smoked ham and cherries, the beer and cider we had at the Democratic rally every fall. "Put the scribbles away, you two. You've got an assignment here: stay reasonably sober and let the mongoose come to us."

The mongoose meant Bill Larkin, though it could refer

to someone else by tomorrow night. But Larkin was an especially likely candidate for names like that. He'd run against my father in his first term, won the primary but lost the general election. Larkin was an assorted flavors businessman in everybody's business; he tried to win our district on a platform of statistics and blue cheese. "He can't win, he's too rich," Ma'am told us. "He doesn't drink," Maury added. "Too ugly," Daddy said, though ugly wasn't quite the right word for Larkin's looks.

But nothing about him seemed too important until after he lost. Then Larkin was always calling my father, asking him on a hunting trip, or saying something snide about him in the paper. Once he called the *Roxbury Review* and told them my father had the worst attendance in the Senate. "Attendance is for schoolkids," Daddy said, and sent the paper a list of hearings he'd held, legislation he'd sponsored. Another time, Larkin sent the governor a case of Jack Daniel's for Christmas: "So you'll understand the peculiar warp in our favorite senator." The governor Federal Expressed the whiskey to our house with a new note: "For another year of revelrous legislation." Larkin even blocked Daddy's membership in the club, then when it went through anyway, he decided to make peace, bought him a set of golf clubs, and asked if his college-age daughter, who was in prelaw, could work part-time in Daddy's office. Maybe he decided it was better, having Daddy at the club, where they could wrangle around in private luxury. On Larkin's ground, not ours. In the kind of place where the hat-check girl looks at the label inside your jacket before she goes to hang it up. I know because it happened to me once, when the lining of my coat was ripped out from soccer practice and Daddy made me give it to her anyway, like I was handing over a silver fox fur.

"You didn't tell me you were bringing the junior partner," Maury said, tilting his schnapps in the candlelight. "Here, Sis, maybe you'll like this better than me."

"Libby's just checking up on us, right kid? Give the evening a little intellectual tenor for a change."

Maury grinned. "Saturday night. Don't teenagers usually go out without their parents on a Saturday night?"

"Not when they're on restriction," I said. "What's your excuse?"

Daddy laughed and Maury smiled like his mouth had been forced with a pair of tweezers. Then I picked up the schnapps, which burned and tingled in my eyes and nose before I even sipped it. I held it there for a second, trying to taste it through my skin, waiting for the antiseptic on my tongue and the childhood diseases in my throat, then pure raw velvet in my stomach. I'd tasted alcohol before, but this was different, thick and sticky, sealing my lips together in tiny patches of resistance when I opened my mouth to cool my tongue. I bent my face into the glass again, and when I looked up, there was Larkin.

His gray eyebrow seemed to jump off into the reckless side of his face, and the thin wings of his nose shivered like the cigarette papers Michael used for rolling joints.

"William," Daddy said.

"Senator."

"Why don't you join us for a couple of drinks, Bill—or soda water, whatever proof you're up to?"

"Yeah, schnapps all around," Maury said, and Daddy took off his glasses and wavered his eyes at him.

"You know my daughter Libby, don't you?" Daddy said, turning back to Larkin. "Libby's a big fan of the democratic process."

Larkin reached across the table for my hand, then barely touched it, leaving a ticklish spot on my palm where it was used to being pressed.

"I believe we met at a brunch. Strawberry waffle parfait. Caviar puffs. Eggs Benedict."

Daddy tapped all ten fingers on the table, like a poker player warming up his cards. "I think the speaker was

18

called that too," he said. "Egg Puff Benedict–something like that."

"I think I remember," I lied. It seemed as if I'd always known Larkin, listened to his daughter Joan do imitations of him in the ladies' coatroom at the capitol, heard stories about him at bedtime, seen his picture on my cereal box at breakfast the next day.

"About your latest travesty of legislation," he was already saying to Daddy.

"Well, I guess you noticed it's a crackdown Sahara spring."

Larkin nodded. "I don't necessarily take that as a sign from God to increase government regulation. Like your Hiawatha Jehovah's Witness friends in high places."

"It's not about God, buddy. It's about seeing more green on a goddamn private golf course than on the corn and wheat we have to live off all winter. Except those of us who're too occupied with caviar puffs."

I widened my eyes at Maury, trying to look knowledgeable and at least sixteen.

"Water bill," he mouthed to me. The creases in his lip stiffened when he said it.

Larkin picked a flower out of the centerpiece and slit the stem with his fingernail. "You belong to the club too, Tom. This one or any other. Because of your service to the people, not despite it. The machine just won't run without the oil of privilege. Or, in your case, the liquor of privilege."

Daddy's face turned white under the eyes, pink at the temples. He put his glasses back on and the two of them just looked at each other for a couple of beats. Like we say in politics, the closer the enemy, the closer the friend. All at once, I knew that Larkin was more interesting to Daddy than Maury or Ma'am or even me. At least for a minute, and that's what I couldn't stand.

"The rain falls on the just and the unjust," I said, without knowing why.

"What?" Maury stopped playing with his napkin ring for that one.

Daddy straightened in his chair. "Yeah, the kid's got the idea. So what about that whiskey? They have a bartender's strike or what?"

"They're on their way, Tom," Larkin said.

"And Maury, dance with my kid here, will you? I want to show her a good time, but she hates how I always sing in her ear. Says I make Willie Nelson sound like church music."

"Sure, Tom."

So Maury and I got up and walked toward the little square of parquet they have for a dance floor. He hooked his hand in the sash of my dress and tilted me into the music, a sad instrumental.

"Yuck, slow dancing," I said.

"Take it easy on your partner, Sis. Besides, you think I'm going to break into the backstreet boogie right here? Not a good career move, I'd say."

"No, but never mind." He was so close his knee nudged against mine at the start of every measure. I shifted to a syncopated rhythm, but that only bumped us together more. "Do you really have to lead all the time?" I said.

"That's usually how it works. What's wrong with you?"

"It's nothing. You're just too—" His cologne kept interrupting me, thick lime over a darker smell smudged onto his collarbone, right where my nose hit. "You're too old to dance with seriously and too young for it to be a joke."

"Well, at least I know where I stand. What's Dot doing tonight?"

"Slumber party. Did you really ask her to marry you?"

He stood still and pulled my face off his shoulder. "Why? Are you jealous now?"

"No. You just shouldn't fool around with a little kid like that. Probably hurt her feelings, eventually."

"Hurt Dot's feelings? I'm only afraid she's going to browbeat my poor old heart right out of my body."

"Don't you ever flirt with girls your own age?"

"Only when I'm off duty," he said. "See, I don't get paid for that."

"Ha." I pinched him on the back, near his left shoulder. But the muscle was too hard and it wasn't very satisfying, nothing like pinching Dot's clingy sponge cake skin when I was mad at her.

"Hey, no abusing the help. It's bad enough being an intellectual whipping boy."

"What do you mean?"

"Never mind."

"Yeah, what do you mean and what's going on with my father and that water deal?"

"He wrote it. He likes it. His friends don't. That's probably all you need to know."

So I stopped dancing and straightened my dress out at the waist. "How come I always get the Disney version of everything?"

"That's not the Disney version. That's the short version. If you want the long version, you have to come earlier. Like about five A.M."

"Let's go back then."

"Why?"

"Well, if you won't tell me anything."

I was already across the dining room before he even cleared the parquet. Then I stopped, listening to my father's political burr, the fancy scalloped edges he got on his voice when he was drinking and talking and making gains.

"And we're not talking kiddie threats here. Rape, mutilation, you name it, it's in there. Right under *L* for lunatic, *C* for criminal, *J* for jail. What I want to know is, are things really that bad? They're down to roping in my kid now? Is that what it is?"

I looked at the candlelight on the table and squinted,

hard, so it made a bright gash over my eyesight. I didn't see anything for maybe half a minute, maybe more, even though I had my eyes wide open now, looking straight ahead. But all I could think of was what my father said, how it all happened because of him. And I know anyone else—and maybe even you—would say I was sad or demented, but I didn't want it to be just my father, not that night.

Just for once, I wanted it to be me. So if I had to get letters like that, if I had to wonder what it would be like to get murdered and pace the whole thing out in my mind, in the mirror, on the dance floor, on the stairs, I just wanted to know it was because of me, myself. The way I walked or whatever. The way I sucked on my ring.

I stepped up and touched Daddy on the shoulder. The table was full now, some people I recognized, some I didn't—all men. And Larkin was gone.

"Tired out?" Daddy said.

"No, it's just that boy. It smells like he's been using gin-and-tonic for aftershave lotion."

Maury came up behind me and they all laughed, most of them thrumming on in an even way, then my father coming in every so often with these clear, chalk syllables almost as sweet as his speaking voice.

Maury pulled out my chair, but I didn't sit down, not yet. Across the table, Daddy pushed his chair out and lifted his glass. He grabbed the napkin off his knee. Then he kissed the thick linen, blowing the kiss off to me.

When I'd finished two glasses of wine and half my chicken, stirred my sherbet around in its real orange shell, picked my seven mints off the dessert tray, Daddy finally decided it was time to go home. He took out his silver dollar Annie Oakley money clip and aimed folded bills at the table, pitching them over his finger one at a time. They landed in a little wreath around the centerpiece, mixed in with the shreds and confetti of flowers Larkin had crumpled around the edges.

In the parking lot, Daddy kept turning his keys over in his hand. Then he dropped them into my palm. "Let's try out that learner's permit, Sly. See if it really works."

"Do we have to?" I was walking with my arm through his, and I tried to wedge the keys back into his rough, broad fingers.

"Come on, Lib, you're always after me to help you practice. Besides, I don't feel so on target myself. That last Daniel's hit me a little funny in the knees."

I unlocked the Torino and got in on the driver's side. On the dashboard, there were three golf tees, campaign buttons for four different senate races, and a red paper flower with "Veterans of Foreign Wars" printed on a tag on the side. The seat was covered with manila folders, rolls of stamps, cans of diet soda, a handheld blow-dryer, a corkscrew, computer printouts, and more mail. I felt something on the floor by the gas pedal, and pulled up a plastic baggie full of fishing tackle–hooks, feathers, and the fluorescent rubber gel of fake worms.

"Present from an admirer," Daddy said, took it from me and lobbed it into the backseat.

Clicking on the ignition, I could feel the engine tremble all the way to my instep, hear its vibrato against my palm.

"Good. You've got it, baby. Eating right out of your hand."

I curved the steering wheel tight and looked out onto the street, where the schnapps I'd drunk was cutting the neighborhood a little crooked.

"I bet you have everything in the world in this car," I said. "Remember that old junk truck Granddad used to have? Sometimes I think your car's like that, only you never sell anything. You just keep getting more junk."

Daddy shifted beside me and crushed some papers up against the seat. "Let me tell you a little secret. He never sold much either."

I jabbed at the turn signal. "Really?"

"No. That was just something for him to do after the heart attack. Get out and dicker with people. Chat them up. Talk them down. You remember how your Granddad was. He gave away more than he sold."

"Yeah, like those Coke-bottle lamps."

"People never understand a guy like that. They think everyone's out to make a killing, and if you're not, you must be a fruitcake or an altar boy. They think they can take you easy, just like that. Then when they can't tag or tackle you, that's when they start to get the shakes."

"Right," I said. "You mean like Larkin."

He pressed the button to the glove compartment and fumbled out more mail. Some fell on the floor and some landed on his lap and some he stuffed back into the open door. "Larkin," he said. "Old Liver Lip himself. You know, he's been after me ever since I was elected. Buy this. Support that. Take this other. Do you believe he was actually trying to give me a tip on some ponies during the state aid push? Ponies. I thought at least it'd be real estate or stock or something with a little silk lining to it. But he's trying to buy me with recyclable racing forms. Christ, Libby, it's not the cheating that bothers me. It's the piddling scale."

I turned onto our street and took the corner wide, jarred over the tight little stomach hill so its billow hit me just right, on the near side of the appendix. Then I swung the Torino up the driveway.

"Home again. I guess I drive OK when I have to."

"You're fine," Daddy said. "That's as good as anyone needs to know how to drive. Any better than that, you're getting too professional."

He opened the car door and bent over the backseat, then dragged out a long strip of yellow plastic that I finally recognized. It was a backyard water slide that Dot and I had when we were little kids. We used to arrange it on the hill, then hook it up to the garden hose and ride down over the lawn all afternoon. I didn't remember when we stopped using it, or when Daddy took it over for himself.

"Tarp," he said, and rolled it out on a flat patch of land at the top of the hill. "I'm not ready to go in yet. What about you, Sly?"

"Well." If I went in, Ma'am would know he was home too, and I figured that was the wrong move. "I guess I'll wait a little while," I said, and knelt down on the plastic.

He settled back with his hands behind his head. In the dark, the lawn didn't look so bad; I could barely see the yellow at its edges. The whole neighborhood sounded wet with silence—just crickets and whippoorwills burbling through the calm. There was the clean stink of dandelion weeds, a furry cloud of pollen, the vague, chemical perfume of the neighbors' weed-eater. Then, underneath it all, the alcohol's hum. A screen door wheezed open somewhere down the block. The wind kicked in and spun the tire of Dot's bicycle lying on its side by the curb.

"Yeah, Lib. Those big money hounds, they need guys like me. They look at you cockeyed, but they need you. Even Larkin, when he's not threatening to go over to the competition. Well, about half the time he's making hand signals my way. And do I ask them to do it? No. But they have to have a Tom Martin, someone spry enough to slip through the cracks. They're all too fat to get in there. See what I mean?"

"I think so." I sat down all the way, so I could feel the uneven lumps of grass beneath the plastic. At this rate, Ma'am was going to hear us, and soon. Or I hoped so, anyway.

"Don't worry, baby. I'll get us through the cracks. You too. You're a slicker, like the old man. Aren't you, Sly? Now listen, Libby. You don't really have to worry. I've got my people on it, OK?"

"I'm not worried," I said. I picked a leaf of mint and laid it over my tongue. "People who write letters like that never do anything anyway. That's why they have to talk about it so much."

"Well, that's one way to see it." He held his thumb up in the light and bit at the nail.

"Ma'am probably wants us to go in now."

"Think so? We'll go in a minute. Just let me get my land legs here."

"Is it really true that she made you call her Ma'am when you first went out with her?"

"Every time, Sly. Tried to get it on the marriage license too."

I rubbed at a snag in my pantyhose and thought about my parents, why they ever got married in the first place. I knew just the person my mother should've met, a tall lawyer who looked a little like a grown-up Michael and whose talk would put Larkin to shame. He'd take Ma'am to the theater and thread his long, brown fingers through the curls at the back of her neck, kiss the wide prickly space over her nose where she plucked her eyebrows fiercely but not often enough. I knew this man so well I drew flow charts of his past love affairs in study hall and picked out his empty seat at choir concerts, when Daddy didn't show. I didn't seem to have any ideas about who should marry my father, though. The truth was, even though he had blond hair and a Jack of Diamonds profile, it was hard for me to imagine him in connection with women at all. Except for Ma'am, that was, and I didn't know what it was with them. Not that I wanted to, either.

But I didn't really care who my father married; I figured it wouldn't make much difference, or have anything to do with me. When I told Ma'am my theories, she said I wouldn't be here at all if she hadn't married him, so I ought to be happy. I could see her point, after all the genetics I had in school. Still, I didn't buy the argument. Whatever happened, I'd still be my mother's daughter, picking mint and reading the Bible, singing musicals and trying on homemade dresses and eating Greek chicken salad at the top of our hill. And this was whether I liked it or not; this

26

was way past what I wanted and on into what I knew.

My one eye felt fuzzy, as if a bug had flown into it. I rubbed it closed and twisted around to check on Daddy, to see if he was ready to go in yet. But he'd already fallen asleep out there on the water slide. One hand clutching his glasses to his stomach. His hair parted the wrong way in the breeze. His mouth was halfway open, as if he'd started to say something, then stopped to make sure everyone was listening first. And I wanted to get it over with and say it myself, if I only knew what he wanted to tell me.

The quiet in the neighborhood turned all tinny, like the pause before the action in a horror movie. I started to admit I was afraid. Only there was no one to tell it to. I didn't want to stay out there alone, but I couldn't go inside and let Ma'am find out about my father. So I sat there getting hypnotized by the lamppost, with its flame shivering high and low in the wind. The tongue of the Holy Spirit. Or just Ma'am trying to signal me from the light switch inside.

She finally came out in a robe and sweatpants, pinching a bobby pin out of her hair. When she saw Daddy lying on the water slide, her eyes turned flat as newsprint. "Just never mind. I knew you were with him all the time."

"We had dinner at the club."

She nodded. "Oh, the sheriff called. He wants you to come in on Wednesday and answer some questions. Fill out some forms."

"But church," I said.

"We'll just drop by on the way."

"Yeah. Well, I had *coq au vin* and Maury danced with me."

She didn't even look after the first time, but her face kept flinching toward my father. "Go in now, love. All right?"

"I don't, I mean–"

"Just go in and try to sleep."

I went in the front door and back down into the basement to try and call Michael on the private line. We first got the basement phone because Daddy wanted to be able to ignore the regular one when he was busy, which was most of the time. So he only gave the new number to family, then his best friends, then the whole long relay race of political cronies. But that got to be almost everyone in town. Soon Dot and I were using it as an RSVP on love letters, and Ma'am was writing it on all her school board forms. Until, by now, we got as many calls downstairs as we did up, and never knew whether we could afford to let anything ring.

"Pedro's Party Palace," Michael said. "You provide the tequila, we'll supply the worms."

"Hey, what's really going on over there?"

"My parents are asleep and we're raiding the bar. But all we've got so far's two bottles of club soda and a lime Grenadier. Big party last night. Mucho cleavage. Mondo beer."

"So when are you off restriction?"

"Looks like about forty-five minutes now. What's the matter, you miss me, Chiquita?"

"Maybe." I poked at some change in a pottery ashtray on the coffee table. "I went out with my father tonight. Dinner and dancing and all."

"Oh boy, big competition for me."

"Well, that's not what I mean." I wondered if I should tell him about the letter. You'd probably like that, I thought. Or maybe you'd rather have me keep it secret, tense and rich and private, like a bone bruise.

"He just felt sorry for me," I said, "because I got this letter in the mail."

"What, did you lose the sweepstakes again? I told you about those things."

"No, it was like a rape letter."

"A what? What's that supposed to be?"

"You know. You're supposed to know all about that stuff. At first, I even thought it was from you."

"What are you talking about?" His voice had a split in it, as if he were edging out a splinter.

"You know, where they tell you what they want to do to you, bit by bit. Then they start all over again."

"God, Libby. You got a letter like that, and you gave it to your father? You said you thought it was from me?"

"Come on, I didn't tell him that. Besides, I knew it wasn't you after a while."

"Oh gee, thanks. Who'd write you a letter like that? Why didn't you call me?"

"What's the matter, you wanted me to read it to you over the phone, so you could get a big turn-on?" I felt my voice rattle out of range–that's when I first noticed I was mad.

"Oh, excellent, Libby. Just excellent wicked. Yeah, that's exactly what I wanted. Maybe you could make a copy for me, huh?" Then the phone clicked off and went into a harsh, straight-edged dial tone.

I hung up the receiver and pushed the phone under the couch. Then I sat down backward, with my feet wedged into the gap between the cushions. Bending back, I let my head hit the floor; the rough, indoor-outdoor carpet scraped against my scalp and I imagined the blood slipping down, blue and unoxidized, behind my retinas. I was definitely mad, but now that I knew it, I couldn't think what else to do about it. I heard my parents arguing upstairs–my mother's logic, fast and efficient as an old-fashioned, clip-on earring, my father's long and friendly blur. There was a knock on the wall, and I felt the vibrations against my forehead. From where I was, I could see the stairs, but no one came running down to check on me.

Just then, the phone rang, right behind my ear. I twisted around, rolled onto the floor, and dragged the receiver out from under the couch. It couldn't be Michael, not this soon. It took at least a couple of hours for Michael to make the turnaround.

On the phone, it wasn't a voice; it was music instead.

Rock music with rats and snarls in it. Like you took a rake and a drainpipe and a hubcap and ran them through the score. Punk, maybe you'd call it. But it was almost pretty. Familiar, too. I didn't even say hello, who was it, just lay there listening, humming, trying to find my chord. I could feel the song swooping and lifting, washing up to the spot where the lyrics would begin. In half a second, someone would start to sing–words, probably some spooky message for me. More than anything, I wanted to hear the words. I thought they would explain it all, not just why you were calling. My mother and father, Michael on the phone. The sad, proud, embarrassed feeling I got when Daddy talked to me. More than anything, I wanted to hear. But more than that, I was afraid. Not so much afraid of you hurting me. Just ordinary afraid. Afraid of making the wrong move, of acting weak or silly or strange. I put my hand over the receiver to keep from saying anything. I hung up the phone. Then I waited until my parents were quiet and the house settled into the hill before I ran, carrying my breath like a descant up the stairs.

iii

In my dream, I was the lion. You were just a boy riding a camel over the beach. "I'm riding to the lions," you kept saying, though there was only me, hiding behind a wet black rock and watching you spit sentences at the waves. Then you got off your camel, walked around the rock, and wrapped my mane around my throat. "You look like a lion," you said. "You look just like a lion when you sleep."

I woke up already talking to my mother, who was folding towels at the bottom of my bed.

"These are for your bathroom," she said. "So I thought I'd just do it in here." She was wearing a shiny striped church blouse and an old beige slip with lace so fine and worn it reminded me of the butterfly wrinkles around her eyes. Ma'am was actual perfume-ad beautiful, not like the mothers of some of my friends, who made up for it by primping themselves poker-faced as magazine covers. She would've liked to be one of those women; I think she even tried. But there'd always be something–the wrong bra or slip, a skirt that bunched up under the waistband, eyebrow pencil too dark for her eyes. It made me itch under the fingernails to see her like that, like that morning, with a crown of wrinkles ironed into her sleeve and her makeup flushing orange where it patched into her seashell-colored throat.

"What did I say?" I asked, pushing my toes under her stack of towels, tilting it over as far as I could without letting it fall. "I was talking in my sleep. First I was out chasing this lion, then I was talking to you. I don't remember what happened in between."

Ma'am flipped over a washcloth and folded it in half.

"You wanted to know what I was doing in your room."

"Oh. Did I say it nice at least?"

"Well, fairly nice. You need to get up now so we can go pick up your sister before church."

I pulled my hobo sleep shirt down over my knees, then sat up and switched on the radio.

"Her friends are so jealous," the Police sang. "You know how bad girls get. Sometimes it's not so easy to be the teacher's pet." Sting's eyebrows even sounded tilted, like he was proud of the story, which was supposed to be a real-life incident.

"Do you think you ought to be listening to that on Sunday morning?" Ma'am said, when I was already in the bathroom.

"Why not?" I turned on the shower, just so I wouldn't have to hear her over the flat splatter of spray.

"It's not exactly spiritual," she said, walking in with the towels. "And besides, your father's trying to sleep."

Then when I got out of the shower and into my dress and hot rollers, the radio was off. So I went in to sit on my parents' bed. Ma'am was standing over by her dresser, holding up necklaces and matching them against the cuff of her blouse. Once she found the right one, I'd have to fasten it on her so it didn't hook the little stand-up mole at the nape of her neck. I always thought of that mole together with jewelry and church-going and etiquette. Then my mother's lawyer lover finding the shivers at the back of her neck. But I still hated fastening her necklaces. It usually took me several tries, struggling with blunt, sweaty fingers, and sometimes she'd tell me I was as clumsy as my father.

Once I finished with her blue Venetian beads, I turned back around to the bed and leaned over to kiss Daddy's cheek. "Happy God-day," I told him. He smelled like the milk carton Ma'am had been keeping under the sink for vegetable peels ever since the garbage disposal broke the year before. That and the strong, expensive sheen of alcohol. His ears were bent a little at the tops, the way Dot marked her pioneer books and plantation romances to keep track of the sickly parts. And tiny diamonds of dandruff showed under his brushed blond sideburns, all fresh and pale beside the raised red skin. It was strange, but when Daddy seemed most disgusting was when I liked him best. Safe and strong-smelling in bed like that, he seemed more like a father, and I could love him with all the steep, adolescent sides of my heart.

"Tell the old guy I'm voting *in absentia*," he said. He sprang open his trick blue eyes and closed them again so fast I couldn't be sure whether it really happened. "I'll go with the expansion of the universe. A bang, not a whimper. Even the head honcho has to stay on the move."

I looked at Ma'am and she signaled me to leave him alone.

"It's pledge Sunday for the missionaries," I told him.

"Yeah, those Christians are some of the biggest money people I've seen. Your mother doesn't know this, but I used to want to be a minister. That is, before I found out how many accounting courses they have to take. That just about did it for old Two-penny Tom. Yeah, Larkin there's a big Episcopalian. I bet you didn't know that. Business and religion and politics, boy. I'll take politics, thanks. It's a little cleaner, overall."

Then he faked a long, crackly snore.

"All right, Tom," Ma'am said. "We'll leave you to get your own religion. Whatever you call it now."

"Sleep. I call it sleep. The closest communion with God there is."

She pushed her scarf drawer closed with the flat of her hand. "Just sleep then, and leave us alone."

"Now I'm going to get it," I whispered to him when she left the room. "The trickle-down effect. She's mad at you, but you're too obnoxious to yell at, so I get the leftovers."

He reached over the bedspread and clutched at my fingers without opening his eyes. "You aren't going to go off and be a Christian, are you Lib?" His lips made a smart, hard squiggle.

"I guess I already am. Since I got baptized and all."

"Oh, that doesn't count. Your old man's baptized too. Everybody gets that done to them, sometime or other. It's how you deal with it that matters. Whether you let someone else tell you what to do."

"Well, maybe," I said. "But you have to let people boss you around when you're a kid anyway. Sometimes, God doesn't seem all that different from Ma'am or my geometry teacher."

That's what I said, but I was secretly thinking about dying and heaven and hell. Heaven was trees with tinsel all year round and no midterms and no dry spells and no elections. When I thought of hell, though, it always looked like the dark place beneath the bleachers on our football field, where kids stood with their hips pressed against the tall metal legs of the stadium, rolling joints in pages torn from comic books and looking up under ladies' dresses during "The Star-Spangled Banner." Once when we were down there, Michael tucked his hand up under my T-shirt, not grabby or anything, more like the way Dot and I used to reach into the refrigerator to touch the pitcher of iced tea when the house was really hot. Before I pushed him away, I let myself feel just that first star of pleasure, like a note too high to hear. And I couldn't get over it; I wasn't so sure I even remembered it right. I always thought boys wanted to touch us because of their weird warts and hormones. I never thought I'd feel something too.

That was the part where the dying came in. Would I have to die before I got there, to the very edge of the feeling? And if I did, would I get the chance to make up for it later? Or once I got to heaven, was that really it? I thought no, and wanted God to kill me while I was still shivering in the scales. I thought yes, and tried to make myself promise to sit up on the bleachers all the way through track and field. Then I even went and thought about you, whether you ever saw me down there under the bleachers and how you got all your smart ideas.

"Well," Daddy said. "Go do something nice for your mother. She's not such a Miss Gloria Morning Star today."

"What am I supposed to do about it?"

"Go cut up the fruit on her yogurt, or dust the living room furniture. She always likes it when you do that."

I kissed him again, this time on the side of his chin with the rubbery white scar where his cousin once tried to shave him with the lid from a can of pork and beans. Or the rose slipped out of his teeth. Or Ma'am kissed him too hard while she was still wearing braces. Or maybe all three, if you listened to him long enough.

"Bye," I said, and he smiled out at me from inside his sleep.

"Go and get her, Sly."

But it was already too late. In the bathroom, Ma'am was undressed again, bent over the bathtub in her slip, with her bruised knees kissing the tile. She had out the Comet and a scrub brush, and as she worked, her hips shook and her calves shifted. The hairpins clicked together at the sides of her face.

I picked at the striped blouse hanging from the doorknob. "I thought we had to go."

"Well, someone in the family has to keep things straight."

"So you're cleaning out the bathtub? Is that supposed to fix our warped religious values or something?"

She didn't say anything. The porcelain squealed under the scrub brush, the way it did when she got rough. That's the funny thing: the more serious she was about scrubbing, the more it came out sounding like a question.

"Hey," I said. "You married him, not me."

She turned around, and before I saw her expression, I felt the scrub brush skim my leg.

"What makes you think it's just your father? You know, Libby, you're part of the family too."

"I know, but I'm not a voting member," I said, and went back to my bedroom, grabbing the hot rollers out of my hair, even though it was too soon.

"I figured out how to get him," Dot said when I picked her up at Melissa Hartford's front door. "We're going to do this video of you in the shower then show it in the library and see who stops to watch."

"You didn't go to sleep last night, right?" I said. "Is this all your stuff?" She had a purple knapsack, a stack of teeny-bopper drool magazines, a green stuffed dog named Ivan, and a Duran Duran album all stashed under the hat rack in the hall.

She twisted her lower lip into the upper one, then reached in with a finger and pulled apart the smile. "Some of the *Tiger Beat*s are Melissa's, but she said I could borrow them overnight. Who'd you rather marry, Sting or Simon Le Bon?"

"No one. I don't want to marry anyone right now. Is that all you think about?"

"No, I'm trying to think how I'll nail this letter guy, only you don't want to talk about that either."

"That's because you're not supposed to know about it. You're too young for that too. Why don't you think about– junior high pep club or something?"

"You know I quit the pep club. It's too preppy for me. Besides, you can't even sit with any boys during the game."

I picked up her knapsack by one strap. "That's what I mean about you. Anyway, don't say anything obnoxious to Ma'am, OK? She's already mad enough."

"With who?"

"Me, then Daddy. Or Daddy, then me. She was taking it out on the bathtub again."

"Uh-oh. Better get me my shades."

"Yeah, that'll be good. I'm sure that's going to get her in a better mood."

Dot grabbed at the flap of her knapsack. "Well, yeah, but at least this way I can cross my eyes at her while she's yelling at me."

"Just button your skirt, all right? Your Supergirl underwear's showing all the way to Santa Fe."

"That's the leggy look," Dot said, and pushed her pink-and-black plaid sunglasses up the wide, solid bridge of her nose. Her hair was tied together on one side of her head with a piece of aluminum foil braided through it, and her eyelids flashed like small change at the bottom of a wishing well.

"Morning, Sunshine," she said, and crossed her fingers behind her back. Then she shifted Ivan over one hip and shoved into the passenger seat.

While me, I was happy just to sit in the back and watch myself trying to look neutral in the rearview mirror, with my hair turning blonder in the sunshine and cardboard-colored in the shade.

"Have a good time, Dottie?" Ma'am asked.

"Not bad." Dot pulled a popcorn shell off Ivan's neck.

"Caterer and a live band type affair?"

"Just Melissa's brother," Dot said. She twisted back to hand me one of the magazines, trying to get me to look at Sting, I think. "He was playing this kazoo and he emptied the spit into my Coke."

"Sounds good to me. Maybe we could get him for your dad's next reception."

"Yeah," Dot said. "We could probably use the bucks. I mean the ones we'd save. You just have to buy Loren a nerdsickle and he's yours for life."

I flicked through Dot's magazine; it was thin and cheap and reedy as a comic book or certain religious tracts from the less respectable churches. All except for a few glossy pinup pages that looked like they were coated with nail polish.

"Is this the new one?" I asked.

Dot turned around again and rolled her eyes. But with her, it looked like they were going to keep on rolling forever, tossing long passes at each other then lobbing them back again. "This week's allowance," she said. "Already gone."

"I thought you were going to buy that sheet music for us."

"Well, we went to the mall last night with Melissa's brother. And you know, I don't like people watching me buy that musical stuff. It's like when you're eleven and someone comes over and sees you playing with dolls."

"What's wrong with musicals? They're a lot more mature than these guys. These guys never did a serious job in their life."

"Sting and Billy Joel are real grown-ups. They're almost as old as Daddy."

"Then they're too old to trust," Ma'am said, and flicked her turn signal on. "Dot, will you please take that oven liner out of your hair now? I think it's had its full effect. Besides, it's not very appropriate for church."

Church was a plain auditorium filled with long pews the color of prairie wheat in a good year and a flat beige carpet that sent snaps of electric shock up into my dress and pantyhose. No organ, just a metal pitch pipe and the pure green tenor of the boys in the pew behind me, that gave me the exact same shivers as eating an unripe mulberry in my backyard. When I got bored, I went through my old pink Bible, with the notes Dot and I had written each other the Sunday before zippered up inside. I'd had the book so long the gold on the edges was wearing white, and I could remember, from when I did such things, that if I licked the red ribbon page marker, it would taste of baking soda. In front of the auditorium, the pulpit was tall and broad and carved with a geometric design that reminded me of an upside-down angel, or Peter hanging tipped-up on his cross; above us, the bare rafters curved like the beached bones of a fishing boat; and when I was beneath them, everything felt turned over under my ribs. I sat peeling rock and roll stickers off Dot's purse, staring at the narrow panels of dark, garbled glass in the windows, trying not to picture the apocalypse.

Dot and I were sitting away from our mother, in the upper left-hand corner of the auditorium, known as the young people's kingdom. We didn't sit with anyone in particular, since we didn't really like church kids, and they were suspicious of us because our father wasn't a Christian and we used big words and missed church sometimes for a benefit or play or opera. But we always sat in the young people's kingdom regardless—we were entitled to it.

In front of us, Holly Anderson was picking hairs off the collar of Eric Ryder's Sunday jacket. I watched her twirl each one around before she finally nabbed it between her prickly pink fingernails then flicked it off into the warm, dusty Sunday air that you could see everything in, all your neighbors' motes as well as your own.

Dot pulled a visitor's card out of the songbook rack and started writing. Then Holly finished, wriggling her shoulders for Eric to help her out of her blazer while Dot passed the note over to me. "Name: Oliver Twist," it said. "Occupation: pickpocket." Under "I would like," she'd checked:

a free Bible ~~study~~

a home ~~correspondence course~~

Other: <u>a job</u>

I shook my head and wrote, "They're doing it again," nodding toward Holly and Eric.

When the note came back, it didn't say anything else. I looked at Dot and she started massaging her purse, finding invisible hairs on it and slipping them into her skirt pocket. I was laughing from my stomach up, trying not to make any noise. Then Brother Dean came up to lead the singing and I put the note away.

"Number 107," he said. He dropped a single note into the room and a canopy of music pulled up out of it. I could feel the notes stretching apart and the parts coming together and the whole song getting built. Only it wasn't a plain house, the one we built on Sundays; it didn't look anything like our church. French doors and bay windows. Slanted ceilings, swirling stairways, landscaping like Sleeping Beauty's lawn.

Dot was teaching me to sing tenor, one octave up. That was a status thing for the girls in our church, once the soprano got too easy. Besides, it sounded better, gave me a ticklish feeling in my nose that spread out over my entire face by the second verse. I thought we sounded better than the boys anyway, only not so spooky, and I hoped that Holly Anderson could hear us up there in the third row.

"What's Ma'am choked up about?" Dot whispered, when 107 was done.

"We were out late last night," I wrote. "Then we were up early cracking on God."

She licked her pencil and started in on the back of the card. "Why do you do that stuff? Especially when I have to come home today?"

"I don't know," I wrote, then flashed the card at her and zipped it up inside my Bible. "Michael's mad at me too," I whispered.

"Boy, you're getting to be more popular than Daddy," she said, too loud, so that Eric turned around to look and the twelfth-grader behind us tapped her on the shoulder.

Dot turned fluorescent pink and crossed her eyes, then folded her fingers together in a church-and-steeple knot.

It was Eric's turn to read the scripture. He whisked up to the front with the cuffs of his suit pants whispering togeth-er. Then he dipped into the verse, in a voice much deeper than the one he used in Sunday school: "Be sober, be vigilant; because your adversary the devil, as a roaring lion, walketh about, seeking whom he may devour."

The lion from my dream. It came out of my dream. Now I remembered reading about him in the Sunday bulletin for the week. And wanting to read the scripture; I could've done a much better job than Eric.

But by the time I looked up again, he was gone and Reverend James was standing behind the pulpit, rubbing his hands over a big black Bible. He didn't even have to read it anymore; he knew the whole thing by feel.

"Today," he said—slow—the way he always started. "Today many of us don't recognize Satan. We've become too sophisticated for that. When something goes wrong, we say society's built crooked, or somebody's psychology isn't on straight. A gang of toughs kills a young mother and her three small children, a husband strangles his wife and abandons her body in a plastic bag along the side of the highway, and we decide we need to build better housing projects or set up more counseling services. Now, I don't believe any of us want to turn our backs on these good works. But we do have to realize that evil is a real force before we do anything about the problems of the world. I'll say it again. Evil is real. Evil is real, despite what the psychologists and sociologists and politicians will tell you. You can see it, smell it, lay your hands on it. The Bible tells us Satan is big and loud and fierce as a lion. And I don't know about you, but I'm probably going to notice a lion running at me in the street. I'm going to notice and then I'm going to do something about it. And it's not going to be just a call to the Humane Society, either."

A few people laughed—Sunday laughs, that came out sounding more like coughs.

Then Reverend James went on to chase the lion, surround it, stab it, catch it in nets. The more exciting the fight got, the more he strayed from the pulpit, stalking and snapping, until he was taking up the whole stage. A tic in his throat began winking at us. His forehead was moving more than his lips, and his wrinkles worked up into the shape of a yawn. Or the roar of a roaring lion, maybe. I was afraid all right; it wasn't like I wasn't afraid of the Devil. But I was more afraid of God. If the Devil was a lion, then God was more like an octopus; he didn't eat a person up, he just squeezed until they were completely gone. Like you. Weren't you afraid of God? Ma'am said you weren't, but I always thought I knew better.

Soon, the spooky part of the sermon was over, and we got to the pep talk about going out and getting on it for God. You know, where the preacher makes saving souls sound like a bunch of kids out selling magazines. Even if I didn't believe it, the guy still got me going. I always knew when the sermon was about to end by that edgy feeling of ambition in my stomach. Though I never knew what I was ambitious about–there was just this blank paper ache. But it was a good ache, like a new cavity at the back of my mouth, or jeans that were too tight in just the right places.

We stood up for the communion hymn, and Dot started shaking beside me.

"Stop laughing," I said. "I'm going to choke and die and get us excommunicated if you don't stop it right now."

Dot zoomed down off a high C and into a whisper. "I'm not laughing. I'm falling off my shoes. My foot fell asleep."

Then we were sitting again and taking communion, thinking about the wrong sort of thing. At least I was. I started out all right, with Christ and the cross and the blood and the body. I held the grape juice in my mouth until it turned bitter with spit. Christ never got hate letters, I thought, but he did know what they were going to do to him ahead of time. This body which is broken for you. I chipped off a piece of unsalted cracker and wondered how he felt about it, if he was really scared, or just sweated a lot in the garden to make it look good. Then I wondered if these crackers actually tasted like the body at all, or if it wasn't closer to the sweet, rubbery gel of my cuticles, when I chewed on them in school. That was more like it. The body. They were always talking about it here. The body of Christ. The body of the church. Whereas when I went home the body was just something policemen found at the scene of the crime. Or boys stared at in magazines. Or Dot pointed out at the country club pool. Then there was the legislative body that Daddy was always complaining about. "I don't know how there can be so many asses in just one body," he'd say. Lots of people said "ass" when they meant body. My ass is in trouble; she's going to get my ass. And Jesus rode into Jerusalem on an ass.

Dot squirmed beside me. She pulled her leg up onto the pew and twisted her foot around so she could look at the sole. "Feels like splinters," she said, rocking and holding the foot with both hands, flexing her toes in a creepy-crawly rhythm.

Watching them, I thought of another thing, what you said in your letter, pushing doors open with my ass. I felt a chill shimmer across my back and shoulders, then blossom into broad daylight at the bottom of my spine. I swallowed the last of the grape juice anyway, and felt my mouth turn sharp and chalky wherever your taste hit.

iv

At home, Daddy was sitting on the front steps in a yellow Hawaiian shirt and cowboy boots, cleaning his glasses frames with silverware polish. Dot walked up to him and bumped her green stuffed dog against his shoulder. "Hey," she said. "What are you doing up?"

He smiled, then frowned and clenched his throat muscles, muttering something about Larkin.

"Larkin?" I said.

"Larkin?" Ma'am asked from inside the screen door. She was already getting changed out of her church clothes and her voice sounded like she was taking off the question and setting it on the top shelf of the closet along with her Sunday hat.

"Maury called and gave me the tip-off. Looks like Larkin's trying to match his tiddledywinks against the big timers again. So I'm thinking I'll give him a chance to confess. But before I get to the door, I have to talk to his kid—Joan's kid brother, who's out there mowing the lawn. Kid comes up to me wearing his pasty-face smirk and asks me, he says, 'How's your drinking arm, Senator?'"

"You went over there, Tom?" Ma'am came back to the doorway and looked out, holding the door open with her foot. She had on the blue shorts again. "You didn't go over there, did you?"

Dot scooted along the porch railing, then lifted herself up onto it, bunching her skirt up behind her. "You did, didn't you? You went over and licked old Liver Lip in the chops?"

Daddy put his glasses on and smiled a short, jerky smile. "Nope. Not the old man. No, I just got Larkin mad enough and let him spill his sleazy guts into the hidden microphone."

He reached into his shirt pocket and pulled out a tiny tape player, the one he usually dictated into.

I was standing at the bottom of the stairs, zipping and unzipping the cover of my Bible. Don't tell me what happened, I thought, because I felt a greasy lining in my throat, as if I already knew. "Dot's too young to hear all about that."

Daddy looked up at Ma'am, his finger cocked over the "play" button.

"Just save it," she said. "Dot, why don't you ride over to Maury's? He was asking about you yesterday."

"But I still have to get my junk out of the car."

Ma'am swung the door open wider. "Don't worry about that. You can always do it when you get back."

Dot arched her back and hopped off the railing, clanging her ankle bracelet against the cast iron as she went. "OK, later Sherlock. But I'm going to find out anyway. I can read lips now, you know."

She ran down the stairs, over the driveway, to the street. She'd woven the tinfoil back into her hair, looser this time, and the silver hit sunlight all down one side of her face, sending camera flashes over the lawn. At the curb, she picked up her bike, stubbed her toe, nudged at the kickstand. Then she was up and pumping down the street.

"She shouldn't be doing that in a dress," Ma'am said. "We've got to start thinking about these things."

Daddy shook his head. "All right, Paula. Lay off the baby now."

She balanced the door against her fingertips, pushing it open, then catching it again, waiting until we both got up and followed her inside.

"Well Paula," he said. "To tell you the truth, I think Larkin may be the bozo sending these notes." He dropped onto the brown velvet sofa Ma'am reupholstered herself when we got old enough to be responsible and Daddy stopped smoking in the living room.

Ma'am settled on the arm. "What makes you think that?"

"Look, he's done everything else. And I'm getting wise to his style. That Rotary Club politics. The homegrown, unfiltered stuff."

Ma'am tugged at the fringe of the Oriental carpet with her bare toes. "Well, what did Maury say?"

"Says the sheriff's office has initiated some research. They sent some detective over to interview Larkin."

"And what does that mean? They'll probably send someone over here too. This is the only town I know where the community leaders and the criminals are on the same hit list."

Daddy moved closer to her, and touched a blue bruise as pale as eye shadow over her knee. "You'd be surprised, Ma'am. In American politics, it's always the same thing. The criminals are better financed, that's all."

I moved farther into the living room, sat down on the rocking chair, and started racing it as fast as it would go, just to hurry up the conversation. "I don't think it's Larkin," I said, but no one paid any attention to me.

"Why not, Sly? Don't you want to find out, anyway?"

"I just don't think it's him. He didn't even remember my name."

"Well, that kind of thing can be faked. Never underestimate the stealth of an unsuccessful operator, Sly. Anyway, I want to find out for sure. I'm not going to sit around waiting for the jury to come unhung on this one."

"So you went over there," Ma'am said.

"I just happened to drop by. Now, you know you don't have to worry about it, Ma'am. Paula. I'm not a violent guy."

I tucked my heels back under the rocker and stopped in midswing. It was true, Daddy had hardly ever spanked me, and never since I turned ten. He always told me he'd stop when I got to be ten, and he kept his promises too—people should remember that about him. But he still lost his temper, until his face turned white under the eyes and red over all the main ridges. He clenched his strong, boxy teeth, so that I could hear them gristle together, like the zipper on my Bible. But worse than that, he didn't make sense. Mad, he couldn't even argue with an eighth-grader like Dot, much less our mother. So we wondered how he did it in politics, in the Senate. Ma'am said he just didn't try to fight when he was in that state, and Maury said he yelled at the help first. I don't think anyone really knew how he thought, mad; he clamped it all shut inside his square manila teeth that never got cavities, no matter how many times he skipped the dentist.

But right now he was still rational, and telling his story: "Anyway, the kid's out there mowing the lawn with his shirt off, trying to mow me down. But I don't bother with the kid, see. I go straight for the monkey meat old man. When I knock on the door, he answers and says, 'Come on in the kitchen, Tom. I've got something to show you.' Know what it is? Know what he's got there, Sly?" He looked up and tapped his fingers on Ma'am's leg.

"It's one of those gourmet coffeepots. Big time green fiend, and he's so excited over this little chrome teakettle his ears are sweating. No kidding. Little green drops, like Ma'am's jade earrings that I bought for her. 'What do you say, Tom?' he asks me. 'Want a cappuccino?'"

"'I want to take a good look at your penmanship,' I tell him. 'I want your ass in a teacup.' Then he starts in. He tells me he's too busy to write letters, business flourishing and all—he always uses a Dictaphone. 'Yeah buddy,' I said. 'I'll ask the police about that. It's going to be a dry spring for you, fellow. Very dry. You'll be sucking on last year's snow tires before it's all over."

"Oh Tom," Ma'am said, and I saw her face shift into a tighter gear.

"And that's when he said all this bunk." Daddy took the tape player out again and rubbed at the volume knob with his thumb.

Ma'am gave him an ugly smile, like she was eating Brussels sprouts, or talking about someone in the next room. "You forgot one thing, love. Whoever you play that for is going to hear you too, and I don't think that's going to be a very pretty speech either."

I got up, leaving the rocker swinging behind me. I didn't want to hear the tape. Not even if it had a clue in it, especially if it had a clue. I didn't want to meet you that way, with four or five other people between us. Besides, I couldn't stand for someone to just spit into a tape recorder, then send me the whole story, like a jewel in a box. I wanted to find out by myself.

In my room, I blew on my mirror, pressed my cheek against the cool glass, and pulled my shirt off over my head, so that my hair made the insect sounds of electric static and stray strands fizzed up around my face. I picked up a magazine off the stack on the floor. I'd already read all the good articles in *Time*. The only ones left were about men and machines and diplomacy, the stuff I tried to skip over in life. I held the magazine flat and shot it like a discus, aiming toward my bookcase at a tall Japanese doll my mother ordered me out of a catalog when I was eight. Near miss. I picked up the magazine and tried again, knocking one of the doll's fingers out of alignment this time. She was holding her hand in that special Oriental curve that's supposed to be seductive–that says "Come here" and "Go away" and "Look how each little bit of me is as precious and exquisite as a snowflake." But now it just looked like she was giving someone the finger, and that made me happy, for a change.

I went into the bathroom, sat down, and checked the thin cotton crotch of my underwear. For the past few months, I'd been finding a warm white paste there that reminded me of elementary-school art. Only the smell was wrong– different–like the clove cigarettes the popular girls were always smoking in the west corridor lounge. It was frightening and sickening and a little impressive, and it happened all the time I wasn't having my period. White, not red. I thought—you know what I thought—that I was turning into a boy. Not a boy really, but one of those people with the characteristics. Still, I didn't find anything there that afternoon and I was disappointed and relieved, wondering if you knew about this and that's why you picked me, or if you didn't have any idea, and it was the one thing that would make you stop.

I stood up, washed my hands, and twisted open the lid of my talcum powder so a chalky haze shot up and made me sneeze. Outside in the hallway, Ma'am was dumping out the clothes hamper with a thick Sunday thud. Daddy had turned on some sports game: I could hear him crunching ice while he watched—a long, satisfied pause and then a shocking crack, starting back at his ticklish lower molar and working all the way into his smile.

In most families, it's the children who leave. They get older, buy clothes too racy for their hometown, and store up hormones like sleeping pills until they have enough to make a fast, smooth break into the outer world. Meanwhile, the parents melt into a middle age that won't peel off the coffee table, that smells of wet dogs and sounds like a mumbling TV that's never turned up or off, either one. But Dot and I were the people in our family who stayed, at least for a while. Through meetings and conventions, years of legislative hearings, school negotiations, cocktails and teas. We were the ones who knew when the mail came every day; how to tell the difference between real danger and the dying bird noises the refrigerator made at night; where to find the old architectural plans hidden in the basement, the scissors or the phone book or the postage scales. We knew how good the cold air coming from the front door feels when it means someone's home early, and how the snow falls off their boots in heavy, flat flakes that melt onto your stocking feet like a love too real and humiliating to remember.

Even more than Ma'am, Daddy was always leaving home. He had an apartment in Baily, the state capital, and kept some kind of scorecard, when he'd be there and when he wouldn't. A plan as intricate as a sonata, so complicated the Russians couldn't uncode it, much less Dot and me. So when he stuffed some socks into his suit pocket, told Ma'am she should've had more heathens for breakfast, and jabbed open the screen door with his elbow, we were never sure whether it was just a dramatic exit or a real jailbreak—an undisciplined puncture wound in the score.

Take me with you, I wanted to say, and I knew Dot did too, just by the way she scratched her calf with her foot and looked out the picture window, down the hill at the schoolyards and stockyards and colored layers of sky.

We didn't say anything, though. Taking sides would be undiplomatic, and besides, we'd have to stay with Ma'am whatever happened. I pulled hard at a hair on my arm just to keep from talking. A car ticked by in the street—someone driving slow, looking for an address. My father would go out and let the screen door whinny shut by itself, then we wouldn't see him again for a couple of days.

You don't understand. You were from people who wanted to settle, pioneer, clear a space and rise in it. We only wanted a place of departure, a plateau where we could get a good running start downhill. But that's where I don't understand either: the one time my father let me leave with him, I didn't want to go.

"Then wake her up," Ma'am said in the living room, sometime between Sunday night and Monday morning. "Tell her you're going to kidnap her and head for the coast."

"Come on, Paula. I'm not hustling you. I just don't want her here alone with that maniac still on the lam. No one would expect her to go in today after what happened this weekend."

"Well, I would."

"I know. That's why I'm taking her with me, damn it. She's ahead in school anyway."

Ma'am turned her voice up so I couldn't pretend to be asleep anymore. "Libby, get dressed. Your father's taking you to Disneyland."

"I've already been," I said, and flexed my hand under the pillow.

"Hey Slick, we want you to take a little vacation and come with me."

"What time is it? It's the middle of the night, and my hair isn't even curled."

"That's politics," Ma'am said. "You get to spend lots of time getting dressed in the car."

I got up and dumped the books out of my knapsack, making as much noise as I could. Then I knelt down by my dresser and stuffed in whatever I found: three tapes, a T-shirt my grandmother gave me when I was in the sixth grade, a skirt, jeans, six pairs of clean bikini underwear, a tube of blue mascara I'd never used. I hadn't been down on the floor like that since I read your letter, and I swiped at the space underneath the dresser just to make sure there wasn't another clue waiting there for me. My fingers came up covered up with a film like a mixture of hairspray and talcum powder; with me, it was a matter of pride not to sweep under the furniture. But the only other thing I found was a chewed-up pen cap, from the last time I did home-work in my room.

"Bring a book," Daddy said. "Your mother wants you to keep up with your studies while you're gone."

So I packed the pen cap too. I'd buy some cheap paper-back on the way.

"Where are we going?" I yelled. "What do I have to wear?"

"Oh, I thought we'd put in a little time at the state build-ing, then head out to the western part of the state for a hearing they're having out there."

"What do I have to wear?"

"Not jeans, that's all I care about, Sly."

I jerked a blue, silky dress off its hanger, then grabbed on my nylons, wad, wallow, wad, wallow, the way I'd always seen Ma'am do. As usual, they wound up twisted around my legs like tomato vines on a stake, but I was in no mood to go back and start over.

Picking up my shoes, I headed down the hall for Dot's room. She curled away from me when I came in, then flipped over onto her back and opened her eyes. Her hair had flattened out in the night, and she looked like an otter with her small, fishy nose and the slight sheen of oil on her round forehead.

"Don't tell me, it's a midnight mass," she said.

I sat down on the bed to fasten my shoes.

"We forgot to vacuum behind the couch. We left the light on in the bathroom. What is it?"

"Don't worry, you don't have to get up," I told her. "I'm going with him."

"Where?"

"Baily, then some hick hearing."

"You get to miss school?"

"Hey, you want to go instead?"

"Maybe. No, sorry. I have French today and I get to do a skit with Jim Conardo. Check back with me on my Tuesday-Thursday schedule."

"Yeah, I'll check back if I ever make it home."

She pushed her head up onto the headboard. "What's wrong with you?"

"Daddy doesn't have any idea about the way we think, if you ever noticed."

"So send him a memo, write an editorial to the newspaper."

"Forget it. I've got to go. I can't believe she's letting him do this."

"Must be part of a plan," Dot said. "Somebody's going to ambush you on the lonely outskirts of town."

"The sooner the better."

"Buy me something from the souvenir store. One of those dolls with the cornhusks. I bet you get some bucks out of it, anyway."

In the living room, Ma'am was putting hooks back into the draperies from the front window. How'd the drapes fall? I thought. She wouldn't lift her eyes off her work. Her mouth looked the same way it did when she was laying out a pattern, holding extra pins between her lips. So that's how it was going to be–I got treated like the enemy, even though she was the one who arranged for me to be on the wrong team.

"Your father's out in the car," she said. "Go on. It's going to be fine. I'll call your principal at school."

"What if I don't want to go?"

"Not your decision. Go on, act civilized. He's just worried about your safety."

"Yeah, who's going to worry about my mental health?"

"I am. Would you just go now? You'll be back by Thursday night. He promised."

"I'm going. I love you," I said.

"That's the easy part," she told me, standing up on a chair to hook the drapes back onto a curtain rod.

I got into the backseat on the passenger side and pushed around the newspapers, clothes, promotional packets, and general junk mail until I was comfortable, then leaned back on my knapsack so none of the buckles touched my head.

"Too intimidated to sit up here with the old man, huh?" he said, dipping his eyes into the rearview mirror and pretending to look at the road.

"Too tired. Just think of me as freight. Like you don't already anyway."

"I think of you as a daughter, if that's OK."

"Sure, if you want to fake it for a couple of days." He didn't say anything. His eyes were out of the mirror now,

54

so it was hard to clock his reaction. But he'd always been a slower steamer than Ma'am.

"I can be as good at it as you can," I said.

"We're a tribe of good ones, Sly. But that doesn't mean there's nothing underneath the act. You've got to remember that."

I couldn't believe it. He didn't go on with a story or a speech or even snap on the radio and make up a bumbly harmony beneath the country nasal of some unlucky trucker from Nashville. He just kept on driving, like he had a plan. The car smelled of expensive alcohol and tobacco mixed in with fast food and dirty socks. I tried to go to sleep, but the smoke stopped my nose up; I had to sit straighter to let the air through.

After twenty minutes or so, the sun stumbled over the prairie, dragging a bleached blond dawn. I stared at the wheat, corn, and soybean fields along the highway. Not that I could tell the difference, not this spring. Everything was just brown and yellow leavings with an occasional thin tinsel of green.

"Pretty sad, isn't it?" Daddy said.

"What?"

"The look of the crop this year."

But I didn't care about any farmer or businessman's profit or loss. I didn't even like the flower garden Ma'am made us weed every summer vacation, sitting sidesaddle on the rough sidewalk in last summer's shorts and digging out roots with our fingernails. I only loved what grew wild, without anyone asking for it: the cool, thick violets in the shade of our backyard, the yellow and purple stinkweed at the side of the road. Still, I didn't even see any blossoming weeds this year.

"Why don't they just use Miracle-Gro instead? Like you?" I preferred my father's farming techniques. For two years now, he'd been digging a trench for his tomatoes and just dumping in the plant food. No weeding for him. The vines grew right out of the grass, and it looked as if our lawn were bearing fruit. "By their fruit ye shall know them," the Bible said. But Ma'am insisted that God counted the method too.

"It doesn't quite work out that way on a large scale," Daddy told me. "But I'll let you suggest it when we get out west."

"Is that what the hearing's about?"

"Yep, you got it."

I picked up a computer printout and tore at its perforated edge. "Is Larkin going to be there?"

"Maybe one of his people."

"What about Joan? Does she count as one of his people?"

"Well, I'd kind of started to consider her one of my people, if you want to know the truth."

"I don't know. I don't think I could ever be one of Larkin's people. Why'd you bring me out here anyway?"

"It's going to be fine," he said.

Already, I could see the greenish noggin of the capitol poking up like a sea monster from between calm gray and blue office buildings. To the right of the football stadium, to the left of the museum. Every time I saw it, I got a slow flash of pride, so cold it made me numb. It was a helpless thing; it happened whether I wanted it or not. And before I could remember how mad I was at my father, I was thinking about our first trip here, when Daddy was sworn in and Dot and I wore our new red cowgirl boots and Ma'am broke in her new professional camera from work. Then all the old senators sang "Happy Birthday" to my father because he turned thirty-four that day.

Afterward, he took us to the governor's office, where we got big blue certificates with golden seals that said we were honorary admirals in our state navy. I wasn't sure I liked that; I saw myself standing at the wheel of a ship wearing an ugly uniform, not knowing what to do. Daddy said there wasn't really any state navy, we didn't even have a coast, but I was still suspicious. Why'd they have admirals, then? Maybe it was just an excuse so they'd be able to draft me later on.

The governor was a big man with black hair in the shape of a Jell-o mold and twigs of broken veins in his face. What did we think about our daddy coming to the big house on the prairie? Did we know what the legislature did? Would we like to sit in the governor's chair?

"Not particularly," Dot said, and the governor blushed as dark and mottled as the rose quartz marble in the panel over his fireplace. Daddy laughed and kissed Dottie on the head. The governor laughed. I laughed. That's when I first remember thinking: they're afraid of us. The old-fashioned radiator whistled and gargled through whole seconds of silence, but Ma'am never laughed at all. They were afraid of us. I couldn't stand to think it; I couldn't stop thinking it. The idea made me feel smart and powerful in the high, fizzy part of my brain, like the foam on a root beer float, but even more stupid and babyish underneath.

Daddy pulled the Torino into the parking garage by the capitol building. "Monday already," he said to the woman in the ticket booth. "Why is it the biggest partyers are always the first ones in on Monday morning? Are we trying to punish ourselves?"

"I don't know about you, Senator, but they pay me to be here this early."

"Well, in my case they hardly pay me at all, so that can't be it. So I must be trying to punish myself."

"That and the car you drive," she said. "If my boyfriend came to pick me up in a heap like that, I'd send him back to the dating service where I got him from."

"Hey, watch the language, Anna. I've got my kid with me today. Do you know Libby?"

"Hey, Libby. You better keep a lid on your dad there. He's like to tear up this little town with his big talk and that mean vehicle of his."

"I know," I said, and considered being jealous, but then decided it wasn't worth it: he paid attention to so many people during a day.

We drove up to the second level, where Daddy had an unofficial parking space. But there was something there already—not a car—some kind of display with a big balloon floating over it. When we got closer, I saw that it was a naked blow-up doll tied by her ankle to a sawhorse. There was stuff all over her—blood, feathers, a pearly stain of toothpaste down one leg. Underneath, you'd made a bonfire out of newspapers and sticks and cornhusks, with a glowing flashlight set inside them for a flame.

Daddy stalled the car. I saw his fist tighten over the gearshift and felt the engine kicking away.

So you knew where we parked now.

But worst of all were the things you didn't plan on: the way she shifted by herself in the slight breeze off the highway, the flat, lipless smile on her muddy face, the happy look of a school project or a nativity scene. Those kinds of art projects had always made me sick, nauseated by the smell of plaster of paris and papier-mâché, depressed at the thought of expressing myself. But that's all I felt when I saw your fancy mess—just thirsty and disgusted, as if I were seven years old and I'd eaten too much glue.

Daddy turned around and put his arm out in front of me, the way Ma'am did when she made a sudden stop. "It's OK, baby," he said. Then he started counting in Spanish, quickly up to ten or so, slower in the teens and twenties, and then back to the beginning. All the time, he was circling up and around the ramp of the parking garage, floor over floor, until I was so dizzy I had to roll down the window and vomit on the pavement. The spirit passing out of me left a slow acid burn like lighter fluid at the back of my throat, and I thought I'd never be empty enough again.

V

"It happened to me," Joan said. She was sitting on a radiator in Daddy's office, her legs stretched out in front of her in textured mauve nylons, and I was at her desk, sipping 7-Up out of a coffee cup, letting each cool bubble burn itself like dry ice onto my taste buds.

Joan laid one hand on her leg and set the other one on the typing table next to her. She moved as slowly as a spy in white opera gloves. "It started up at Lake Arapaho—you remember that."

Four summers ago, Daddy had a weeklong conference there, so we all went, even though Ma'am said we'd be better off just running through the sprinkler at home. Most of the time she stayed by the pool in a sun hat reading books on school management and the philosophy of education. So Joan, my father's college-girl secretary, took Dot and me to the lake, to the amusement park, to the video lounge. She wasn't just an ordinary secretary, but Larkin's real-life daughter, and it showed. She was so thin the strap of her swimsuit stood out from her collarbone, like a bow strung tight. Her breasts were just ripples under the thin, purple spandex. Out at the lake, Joan never wore a bra. She had a trick she did instead, where she stuck skin-colored Band-Aids tight over her nipples and only bit her lip a little if she got the sticky stuff in the wrong place. She had baby blue pulse points behind her knees; her white-blond hair folded onto her shoulders in thick swirls the color of the wedding silver we never used, but kept in a big oak box under the kitchen counter. She wasn't exactly pretty, but so plain and perfect it made my stomach flop over like a fat dolphin to know I'd never grow up that way.

Now she was leaning over and pouring more 7-Up into my cup—her cup—with a picture of Earl Warren on the side. Joan was starting law school in the fall.

"When we were out there Senator Mills started coming around and touching my hair. I hate when people do that. It feels so prickly—like an insect crawling over you at night. Then weird things started to show up on my pillow. I guess he'd gotten friendly with the chambermaid too."

I took another swallow. "Like what kind of things?"

"A lollipop. Silk panties. Even a rubber once." She looked at me closer and her gray eyes seemed to grow one more layer of blue. "Oops, you know what that is, don't you?"

I tested out the rollers of Daddy's office chair. "Sort of."

"A condom?"

I remembered something I heard at a pool party once. "Trojans, right? They have them in the bathroom in gas stations."

"I guess that gets half credit on the sex education quiz. Ask your mother—no—ask your boyfriend. That should give him a little thrill."

"So how did you figure out it was him?"

"Senator Mills? Well, like I told you, he was touching my hair. Besides, you get a feeling about guys like him. Know what I mean?"

I thought about you and your tricks and my scalp stung and itched at the same time, little shivers slipping down my neck like perm solution. I knew what she meant. You probably did too, and only picked girls who'd be able to recognize it. Still, I didn't have any confidence about my guesses. I felt that way about everyone now. No one made the acid oil slick in my throat any stronger or weaker. Not even Senator Mills. My father told a story about Senator Mills at Lake Arapaho. They were having drinks in the glassed-in lobby overlooking the pool and we were laying out in beach chairs. "So, get a look at those dishes out there," Mills said. "Who are they?" Daddy gobbled a couple of olives and told him, "One's my secretary, one's my wife, and one's my daughter." After that, Mills shut up about me and my family, but I guess he kept it up with Joan.

On Sunday of that week, Ma'am wanted to go to church, even though all they had at Lake Arapaho was a nonde-nominational chapel shaped like a tepee.

"It looks like an adventure park," Dot said, and Daddy told us it was pretty close.

"We don't have to go with you, do we?" I asked Ma'am while she was separating her eyelashes with a wet finger-nail. "Please? We're on vacation." I couldn't wait even one more hour to put on my new one-piece swimsuit, still damp from the day before, sticking to me like crepe paper and smelling of minnows and pond algae and Joan's nat-ural aloe suntan lotion.

"What if God took a vacation, Libby? Suddenly, your nose is gone. Your sister disappears. The lake isn't where it used to be yesterday. And you say, 'What's going on?' and God says, 'I'm on vacation.'"

"Shh, you'll jinx me," Dot said.

"Well, I don't mind about the sister part."

Daddy reached over to the nightstand and felt around for the phone. "Let it slide, Paula," he told her. "They're kids. They've got the rest of their lives to sit around churches in tight shoes." He didn't wait for her to answer, but just called up Maury at home and asked him about Mills's track record, if there was anything they could use. He leaned back in his white T-shirt, one hand behind his head, and the hair under his arm made a blond starburst against his red skin. Resting the receiver on his shoulder, he moved his hand down the phone cord, winding each coil over his knuckle and examining it like a jewel or clue.

Ma'am unzipped her dress, went into the bathroom, and turned the faucet on full blast. She wouldn't scrub the bathroom in a hotel, would she? Dot and I looked at each other, indecisive in our pajamas. We knew she was right to be mad; our father wasn't supposed to make decisions about us–we were our mother's territory, her constituents and courts and committees all rolled into one. It was an abuse of power, like he was always talking about. But in this case, he was being more reasonable than she was, so we didn't want to complain.

When Ma'am came out of the bathroom, she was dressed again, and Daddy was still on the phone. She went over to get the hotel key off the nightstand. Daddy looked up to kiss her and she ducked away.

"Enjoy your morning," she said, buttoning her cuffs and shaking her watch down over her wrist. "Don't feed our children too many screwdrivers."

She shut the door behind her with an extra click of the handle. Before the vibrations stopped, Dot and I ran into the bathroom for our swimsuits. But they weren't on the shower rod where we'd left them. The bathtub was filled with soapy water and in it were my father's golf shoes along with dirty socks, two tourist shirts, and yesterday's paper. The black ink was beginning to crawl off the pages and into the water in smoky curls. Scarier than your freak display, really. We sunk our arms down into the water and sorted through the slimy mess for our swimsuits. Then I turned around and saw them hanging from the towel rack behind the toilet–two preteen-age one-pieces, red and blue, turned right-side out, the straps untwisted and the lining straightened out at the crotch and breast. I wished she'd thrown them in too, I thought. So I went ahead and did it myself, while Dot stared at me with her mouth open.

When Daddy got off the phone, we showed him what had happened and he said no hassle, hombres. He pulled the shower closed in short, noisy jerks that pulled up goose bumps out of my arms. Then he called the maid, let us pick out new swimsuits at the hotel shop, and took us to breakfast with Joan.

She had on her swimsuit too, with a long matching jacket. Pockets over the hips and separate panels in the back like the tails of a tuxedo coat. At the table, she kept adjusting the lapels and fingering her collarbone, as if she were reading Braille. Touching the sharp points of the silverware then pulling back again.

Dot shook a mound of sugar onto her plate and rolled a melon ball in it. "Don't look now, but she's back. The mad baptizer. Ma'am the Baptist."

Dot was right. I could hear the scritch-shuffle of Ma'am's good sandals from behind the terrace. But even worse than that was the way my face turned numb in the direction she was coming from, like the sun coming up, only in reverse.

Daddy said, "Why don't you girls go out on the town for a bit?" He handed me ten dollars. "Go on, I'm giving you the chance to make your break."

Joan put down the silverware and turned sideways in her seat. Dot ate one more melon ball. I tucked the money into the top of my swimsuit. Then we walked away before Ma'am got to the table. We went away from the lake this time. Through a patch of woods, past a campsite, into a field of purple thistles where I stopped, stunned, stung in the ankle. A burr was caught in the cuff of my anklet, right up next to the skin.

"Just pull it out as fast as you can," Joan said.

"Yeah, like your baby teeth," Dot told me, even though she cried over every one of hers.

Joan clucked her tongue against her teeth. "You say 'Rumpelstiltskin' and I'll pull it out."

I looked at the spiny green burr, the color of an inchworm. "I think I'll leave it in there for an experiment and see if it falls out eventually."

"Eventually when you get gangrene," Joan said, and bent down and poked at my sock. She smelled like warm butterscotch pudding with the skin still on it. The sleeve of her jacket touched my calf and her silver hair covered everything, so I couldn't see my foot anymore. I pictured my legs anyway: three tweedy, half-healed scabs, a bruise shaped like a tornado with a purple eye, lots of short blond hairs that seemed to grow in different directions ever since I borrowed one of Ma'am's razors and hid out in the junk room of our basement to shave my legs.

"You're supposed to use soap and water, love," Ma'am said when she found me there, wiping blood off the blade of my calf with one of Daddy's campaign brochures. "Maybe you should wait a few years anyway." I'd just wanted them to be clean, the way they were before. But now I was ashamed for Joan to know I wasn't shaving yet.

"Hurry up," I said. "My toe itches."

"Just keep your nose on," Dot told me. "Maybe you're jinxed cuz you didn't go to church today."

"Rumpelstiltskin Jehoshaphat," Joan said, and pulled out the thistle. She stood up and held out her finger to show me the burr resting there, harmless. Then she stuck it to the lapel of her jacket, like a medal, and we walked on to the store.

"Doesn't your mom let you shave your legs?" she said.

I sucked my stomach in. "Well, she didn't say I couldn't. She just made me feel so dumb about it that I didn't want to anymore."

"Hmm. Well, I started when I was younger than you. Some boy showed me how to do it at equestrian camp."

"What's 'equestrian'?" Dot said.

No one answered her.

"It just seems stupid. Cuz once you do it, you can't stop."

Joan lifted her eyebrow. When she did that, she reminded me of her father. "Well, it looks like you already started."

"So what? Ma'am said it's precocious. And we've already got too much of that going on around our house."

Joan laughed. "You do, huh? Is that why you call her 'Ma'am'?"

"No, that's just because Daddy does."

"And why's that?"

I started to tell her, but then Dot interrupted. "It's a family tradition," she said. "He doesn't remember anymore."

By that time, we were at the store and Joan said we could buy whatever we wanted, even if we went over the ten dollars. "I get my allowance tomorrow anyway."

We picked out: two orange-and-green feathered fishing lures, two lipsticks, a thin paper packet of hairnets, a bag of buttermints, an account ledger, and a *Glamour* magazine.

"That's what I like about your family," Joan told us. "You're not greedy–only weird."

Back at the hotel, Joan went into the clubhouse for a sauna and Dot and I took our presents to our room, where we could hear our parents fighting through the wall. Not the words, just the gist of them. Like broken crystal gristling together inside a layer of expensive tissue paper.

"Family fun," Dot said, and bounced on her stomach onto the bed. She twisted uneven knots of her hair into two hairnets, then started playing cat's cradle with the third one.

I just sat down in the chair farthest away from our parents' room. Flicking through our new magazine, I felt it drag open at an especially heavy page, with a free sample inside. A white pad with blue lining, goose bumps embossed onto the thick layers of gauze. I touched it, lifted the sticky underside from the page and made a scraping static sound so that Dot looked up from her hairnet, then turned back again. I knew what a sanitary napkin was from television, and from the boxes Ma'am bought in the supermarket, but I'd never seen one up close before. It seemed wrong for me to be seeing this one too, as if someone had snuck it into my magazine for a joke. Someone. Joan. But it was really just part of an ad that came free in everyone's magazine. A sharp, broken-off piece of my parents' argument poked through the wall. "Breach of trust," I think she said, or "Eat the dust." I brought the magazine up to my face and sniffed the ad. What they call unscented, like Joan's antiperspirant that she let me borrow once. Only it really meant the smell of wind, the open nozzle of a vacuum cleaner, or what comes out of a whipped cream can when the cream's all gone.

Lowering the magazine back down to my lap, I felt bad—guilty—as if I knew more than I should and less than I wanted to. I fished out a black felt-tipped marker from the cushion of my chair, thinking I'd draw a mustache and freckles on the face of the pad. But I couldn't. I wanted it blank, the way I wanted Joan. Because once you mark something, or someone, you can never take it back again. You'll have to remember for always the way you colored outside the lines. Your mother will hang the lopsided elephant up in her office for everyone to see. Or your teacher will send the pinheaded angel to the school counselor for further analysis. Even in my own private diary, there was the same problem. Every year, I'd write about my birthday, and then erase the page. I wanted to save the space under June 12th—I might have a better birthday the next year, after all. But it would always be spoiled by smoky pencil smudges from the year before.

In my parents' room, the argument was tuning up. I could almost put the words together. But I didn't want to know yet what was happening. Because if I tried to understand it now, I'd get it wrong for sure. So I held the whole thing open, blue and white and shaped like an hourglass in my mind, until Joan brought it up again.

"Then what happened with Senator Mills?" I asked her.

She pulled a paper clip out of its magnetic box and unbent it, link by link, over her finger. "Oh, your father called it off. I think they had some kind of whiskey seance over it. Looks like your dad won."

"Oh."

"Either that or Mills moved on to more fertile virgin

territory. He'll be after you next. Hey, you don't think Mills wrote your love letter, do you?"

I shook my head. "He knew what I did at school. He knew what kind of ring I wear."

Maury came into the office with a bag of candy bars. "Cavities for everyone. Compliments of the security staff. All except for you, Judge. Don't want to endanger that precious, ferocious little overbite. You're going to need those fangs."

"Uh-huh," Joan said. "Sooner than you think. Just give me the healthy kind."

Maury ignored her and knelt down by my chair. The part in his reddish-brown hair looked white and moist and unhealthy, like the underbelly of a frog. The skin of his forehead wrinkled and wriggled into two intelligent knots.

"How's it going there, Sis?" he said, and rubbed my arm, hard, quick, like he was trying to scrape something off it.

"Your dad wants you to go down to the floor when you're done eating. Tell the man in the red coat you want to see the Honcho."

"Yeah, I've been down there before. Like about three million times."

"Just reminding you, OK, Sis?"

"She's not helpless and she's not five," Joan said. "I guess she'll go down when she feels like it."

The acid at the back of my throat flared up. I thought of colored sugar water shooting into the veins of a celery stalk, or a run tearing down my nylons. "I'm not hungry," I said. "I think I'll just go now."

Downstairs, a tour was starting up in the rotunda. People and packages and baby carriages were scattered over the tile mosaic on the floor. A skinny blond boy in a muscle shirt stood on Ceres' bare belly. Someone's pretty mother paced around on high-heeled pumps and covered the part of Neptune I didn't like to see–like a bunch of grapes with the leaves still on them. The guide, an old girlfriend of

Maury's, set her hands over her ears as if she were wearing headphones. That was always how she began.

I stayed to watch her point to the carved wooden doors of the courtroom, where an Indian princess held out a peace pipe to a settler. The handles came together where they met. Unity. Justice. Brotherhood.

"Or death," I said out loud, remembering what my father told us about the French Revolution.

A few loose looks fluttered over my way, and Tammy—that was the guide girl—scrunched up her lips. Straightened her string tie. Then went on. The mural over the courtroom door, she said, portrayed a teacher and her students in a famous blizzard that happened in the early years of our state. All you could see, though, were some colors smeared in slow motion through a black-and-white storm. And then, at the corner, a yellow lantern light. The teacher didn't lose a single student in that storm, Tammy told us. She tied together all their jump ropes and made them hold onto the line, walking Indian file and singing church songs until they made it to the nearest farm.

That was my favorite painting in the whole capitol. The one yellow corner and the thick buzz of white. But I liked it better without the story. The story reminded me too much of my mother when she made me memorize our phone number: 731-0132. We had to march around the kitchen—my mother, my sister, and me—singing the numbers to the tune of "Ring around the Rosy" until we got it right. Perfect. Forever. This is what you say if you ever get lost. Tell this number to the policeman, and then he'll bring you home.

"What if I don't memorize it?" I said. "Does that mean I'll never have to come back?" Just one number off, just one little mistake, and I might get to live in another house with different toys, playing with a more cooperative sister. I did memorize it, finally: 731-0132. She wouldn't let me get a Popsicle out of the freezer until I sang a whole verse of it by myself. But afterward, I went to my room, crawled into my closet, pulled out my grandfather's abacus from the Japanese occupation, and scrambled the colored beads so cockeyed I never knew my own phone number again until I was thirteen.

"Three miles in the blinding snow. Pioneer spirit," Tammy was saying as I turned into the senate chambers. A white-haired man in a red coat stopped me at the second double door.

"Guest, press, or general public?" he said.

It was like the Emerald City, only red instead of green. For a minute, I thought I'd have to give him my phone number and considered getting it wrong again, just for fun.

"I'm with Senator Martin. I'm his kid."

"Oh, yes. He said he was expecting you. Are you the one with the pen pal service?"

"That's my sister," I said. "She's younger."

The senate floor was like a wedge of amphitheater tilting down toward the speaker. On the sides were balconies supported by marble columns from three different countries, and the ceiling had the same oak and acorn pattern carved over and over in foot-long blocks. Today, half of the seats were empty. An older senator was standing at the podium reading out of Webster's dictionary while the speaker stood below him at the foot of the railing, giving directions to a long-eyed brunet page in a short red jacket. Of the people who were there, most of them sat at their desks reading newspapers and drinking coffee or soda from Ace of Diamonds paper cups the pages brought them from the snack bar.

Daddy wasn't at his desk. I saw him standing over by one of the columns, his suit jacket hiked up and his hand playing over the nape of his neck. It looked like he was scratching his head, but it was really just a stalling technique. I'd seen him do it before when he was talking to overexcited voters at cocktail parties, or when Ma'am asked him didn't he think it was time to go home yet. The hair straightened out under his fingers, then slipped back into curls when he let it go. His wedding ring came in and out of view.

I put my hand up and caught his fingers on their next pass over his neck.

"Libby," he said, before he'd even had time to turn around. The person on the other side of the column was Larkin, laughing, his eyeballs quivering with the fluorescent gel of cafeteria gravy.

"Libby, baby, are you all right?"

I nodded my head, still looking at Larkin.

"Tell you what, Sly. Go up and tell those barflies in my office to run and get the car. We're going on a road trip."

vi

The car jostled as Maury skidded over the speed bumps, and my stomach pounded up against my lungs. I didn't know why Daddy let him drive. But then, he always got someone else to drive if he possibly could. Once he even had Dot drive us home from the lake when everyone else had sunstroke or a hangover or both. I only hoped I wasn't going to throw up again. Daddy and Maury I didn't mind, but I hated to vomit out the window in front of Joan, who always seemed so clean in every way. She was sitting next to me in the backseat, flipping through a computer print-out with one hand and playing a calculator with the other. I touched the loose silk of her sleeve, just for luck, hoping she wouldn't notice. But she did, and tugged back at my bra strap, then asked me to look up Danitria on the demographics map.

I read it off for her and checked my stomach again. It still hurt, but not bad, just a long, thoughtful pain, like grapes rolling around in a greased wooden bowl. After a while, I realized it wasn't just nausea, I was probably getting my period too. Ma'am told me that I might want to keep track of my cycle, that some women marked the expected date down on their calendar with a discreet *X*, how some girls felt cleaner if they used a douche. Which made it all the more certain I would never do these things. So I never knew what was going on until I was in the middle of bleeding, and already leaking through my clothes.

"We have to stop," I said. I leaned up to tap Maury on top of his head, avoiding the naked part in his hair.

"Sorry. This is the express line. No one stops until we make ground zero."

"I'll tell my father what you said about him and Senator Mills."

"In that case, where do you want to stop?"

"Wherever," I said. "I just want to go to the bathroom."

Daddy looked up from the loose-leaf folder in his lap. "How about a late breakfast, gang?"

"Are you actually reading that?" I asked him.

"It's as close as I get to reading. Line graphs."

"Bar graphs," Joan said. "That would be more appropriate." She pulled a rat-tail comb out of her purse and beat on the back of Daddy's headrest with it. "Personal appearance, Senator. It may be just a greasy spoon, but that doesn't mean you have to look greasy."

"Want to do me up here, Lib?" he said, even though I knew Joan wanted to do it. I leaned over her anyway and combed down his curls, blond at the top with deeper waves of brown underneath.

My stomach gave another roll and jostle while I was half standing, half leaning over the front seat. I remembered the first time I'd felt like this, when I was in the eighth grade and couldn't keep my mind off a certain redheaded boy in my chemistry class who was always trying to copy off my lab reports. He told me girls were space cows and punched my left breast once in the hall and I still liked him anyway. He would do, I told myself. He would do to fight with for the rest of my life. I pictured his hair on my blue organdy pillowcase, thick and tangy and comforting as homemade tomato soup. That was it. I held my stomach and traced over the organs, the ones they showed in the mysterious after-school movies for girls only. When I figured out I was finally going to have my period like everyone else in my class, I sensed a sure victory over the redheaded boy. He'd never understand, and even if he did, he'd only be embarrassed—embarrassed and scared, more pitiful than a girl holding a notebook over her bruised breast in a chemistry lab.

Was that you, I wondered, crouched combing my father's hair on the way to Danitria. The redheaded boy from school. Was that who you were? But you're not afraid of blood, are you? At least, that's what you said.

Maury stopped the car at a place called Happy Trails and Joan got out, then stood in the parking lot pinching her dress away from her shoulders and the backs of her knees. Daddy fussed around in the front seat, opened the trunk, got out a cowboy hat for me and a Greek fisherman's hat for himself, and we all went into the restaurant.

"Four," Joan told the waitress at the register, though Daddy was already headed toward a table. I stood there and waited for the menus with her, just to be polite, though all I could think of was getting to the bathroom before I ruined my dress. Once I made it, I found a dark reddish brown stain in my underwear. My legs shook. My mouth tasted of baking soda and my whole body smelled like the rusting pipes in our garage. Even though this had been going on for two years now, the blood still shocked me every time. It was real blood, not soup, not ketchup, not the sexy pink ribbon of taffy I'd expected. The bathroom had a tampon machine, but those were only for wild women and mothers, as far as I was concerned. So I wrapped some toilet paper around my hand like a bandage and then made a little pad, hoping it wouldn't slip out of the elastic in my underwear when I walked.

Back at the table, Maury was balancing the salt shaker on a mound of salt. "For luck," he said, and shook some over his shoulder at me.

Joan licked her finger and brought a few grains of salt up to her lips, showed the neat purplish tip of her tongue. Then she opened her purse and threw out a deck of cards.

"Spades," Daddy said.

"Go fish," Maury suggested.

"Wrong again," she told them. "My roommate gave them to me. They're tarot cards."

I picked one up and turned it over. A black woman and a white man, back to back, dressed identically.

"The lovers," Joan said. "That's your card. It could mean either fairy tale's end or some kind of complete disaster."

Daddy cleared his throat. "But can we get into a game of cards here, that's the question."

Joan shuffled the deck and the motion lifted her silky bangs, shirred the silk over her chest. "Why not?" And she dealt out a hand.

Daddy won with a suit of wands, but no one told any fortunes.

"Later," Joan said. "When it gets dark."

The waitress brought four plates up to our table, holding them stacked together with lots of tension, so that I could see the cords in her wrist.

"But I never ordered," I said.

"We got you strawberry pancakes, baby. I thought that's what you'd want," Daddy told me, tucking his napkin into his pants.

What I really wanted was just fruit and cereal, like Joan. Although it was true I usually ordered strawberry pancakes. Maury had an omelette filled with a colored confetti of meat and vegetables; Daddy got sausage, eggs, hash browns, toast, and a bowl of Texas chili.

"Chili chaser," he said, picking up the bowl and sipping the first bit down without a spoon.

I looked down at my strawberry pie filling bleeding into the whipped cream. I felt sick again. I didn't want to watch my father eat. I remembered him folding over three thick slices of cheddar cheese and eating them in a sandwich—cheese on cheese. Draining cartons of buttermilk at the refrigerator door. Finishing a whole jar of pickled pigs' feet in a single afternoon of football games. And then drinking the juice.

"I'm not hungry," I said, and twisted my napkin into a knot.

Maury flicked a bit of omelette into his mouth and pointed the fork at me. "And she's the one who made us stop."

"And you're the one who's enjoying yourself stuffing your face," Joan said.

Daddy stretched his hand across the table, but it only reached to my fingertips. "What's the matter, Sly?"

I shook my head.

Maury went on eating while Joan lined up pats of butter around his plate. "How about a little more saturated fat, Buttercakes?"

He stopped for a sip of milk. "Some of us aren't afraid of our appetites," he told her, swallowing, and everyone blinked.

At lunchtime we drove into Danitria, population 1,320: half Indian, half not. The most impressive thing about the town was the water tower, which was shaped like a tin pail and painted with dogs and horses.

Maury parked, dragging on the steering wheel. "Here we are, prairie girl."

"The one they sing about in all the songs," Joan said.

Maury picked up speed again. "This is where that lunatic lobbyist lives, isn't it? The one who asked Tom to come out and see the ark he's building in case the water bill doesn't come through and he has to bring down a flood on our evil generation?"

"Whitehead," Daddy said. "Cyril Whitehead. You know he's going to show up for the hearing. Probably do some ritual snake-wrestling too."

Joan clicked her tongue. "I don't know why you bother with people like that."

"You don't, huh? I bet you don't, sweetheart. That's what happens when you grow up in a house filled with cream puffs and cappuccino machines. This Whitehead's stinking rich. He's a latex monarch. Prince of plastics. And he's looking for creative ways to waste his money."

"Well, he can always waste it on me," Maury said. "I

need a television and a radio in my office for those long, sleepless nights of legislation."

Daddy just ignored him. "Swing a left here and then keep on complaining till the next traffic light."

"Where are we going?" I asked.

"Senator Russell's. Ada's. I figure we'll camp out there while we handle this hearing."

"Do I know her?" I asked, though I was sure I did. She was one of the three women in the Senate, the one who didn't dye her hair, the one who came in the first day of the session wearing dress pants, an embroidered work shirt, and snakeskin boots. On the empty desk next to her, she kept a plastic Hawaiian doll in a grass skirt and a man's white dress shirt in a cellophane package. If anyone commented on her clothes, or acted coy and superior with her, she'd point them one desk down. "Ask the lady in the skirt," she'd say, or "Refer to my stuffed shirt over there." According to Maury, she was supposed to be in love with my father.

Senator Russell came to the door in a quilted satin robe and her boots. Her short black hair was frosted over with a wispy veil of white, heavier over one eye. In her hand was a half opened can of dog food.

"Just feeding my boys," she said. "I thought this was going to be over at the courthouse. What, did you bring your own SWAT team?"

"Media press kit," Daddy said. "Got to keep up with the times. No, you know my regulars, and this one's a little bit of nepotism. My daughter Libby."

"Hey Libby." She switched the dog food to the other hand. Then she pushed her hair up off her forehead and forgot to shake my hand.

Daddy took the can away from her and walked on past into the living room. From where I was standing on the porch, I could see a disconnected bicycle wheel, a lawn chair, a footrest with a tin cake pan resting on it.

"So, Ada, we were scoping out the area and wondering if you'd put us up for the night. In the interest of democracy, of course."

Senator Russell waved us in the door. "Christ knows I'd do anything for democracy. Especially if it's illegal. My firetrap is your firetrap."

Inside, the room wasn't as messy as I'd expected, just filled with pieces that didn't go together: duck decoys, a cribbage game set up on a cork coffee table, peacock feathers and cattails in a wicker basket. The air smelled of meat and pollen and dried things. Behind me, Joan's perfume made a pitiful little trail of flowers into the room. I could tell she was looking for a place to set down her papers for the hearing and didn't like anything she saw.

"Go on, Maury," Senator Russell said. "Find something to entertain these girls. They've had a long drive and they're looking bored."

Daddy was already back in the kitchen. I heard the slosh of dog food flopping into a plastic dish. He was actually feeding her dog, a thing he'd never do at home. Ma'am could hardly get him to put the lid back on the peanut butter.

He stepped into the living room with a bottle of whiskey. "Political maxim number one. You want to smell what's really going on, check in the kitchen."

Senator Russell laughed. "But you have to go in the bathroom for the bathtub gin."

"No gin before the hearing," Maury said. "We have to draw the line somewhere."

"No gin, just whiskey." Daddy opened a china cabinet lined with green felt and poured everyone else a shot glass, then handed me mine in a cracked teacup painted with green and pink roses.

"To Larkin," he said, and I felt the whiskey burn a blush onto my face. Not too good for my stomach, I thought, but it hollowed out a passageway through my guts where everything was cleaner and less confusing.

"Which one did you mean, darling?" Senator Russell said. "Or were you referring to the whole father-daughter team?"

Joan downed the rest of her whiskey. "I'm not part of the team. Besides, it's not my year. I'm waiting for better prospects, not to mention a higher grade of alcohol."

Senator Russell tipped her shot glass and cocked her head to the side, listening for something. "You may be waiting a long time then," she said. "At least until we get ourselves a better irrigation system here in this county." Then she shrugged and turned toward the front door just in time to see a boy with blond ringlets walking through it. He had a wrench and a hammer hanging from the belt loops of his cutoffs, and his tan legs were as hairless and intelligent as a girl's. On the back of one of them was a long white scar—bumpy—like the texture of his hair, and I wanted to touch its strange, pearly seam from the minute I saw it.

"Ada," he yelled up the stairs, before he spotted us in the living room. "Oh, Ada. There you are. Cyril laid me off for the rest of the day. Maybe the rest of the summer. What's the point of fixing an ark like that when the river's so far down?"

"He'll change his mind," she said. "He always does."

"Cyril?" Maury asked her. "You've got your kid working for a religious cracker like that? You might as well just give in and get him a job in the government."

But Daddy didn't act surprised.

"Hey Tom. Hey, Maury. Hey, Joan," the boy said, then dropped down on the sofa next to me. "Hello beautiful lady, whoever you are." He smelled of fish. Fried fish, fresh fish, river fish. Flaky white meat off a rainbow trout. He smelled stronger than me, I thought, which was some kind of comfort at least.

"This is my road manager, Libby," Daddy said. "She doesn't date guys over fifteen or under twenty."

"I'm Tim," the boy said, and kissed my hand, leaving a sticky feel. "I don't date anyone as beautiful as you. Not yet, anyway. They're usually too persnickety."

Senator Russell clinked her glass against the whiskey bottle. "It's a good thing, too. You're untenable as it is. Why don't you go into the backyard and sweet-talk those hounds of yours? Or fix the drainpipe, seeing as it's still working hours."

"Can't a guy take a little break? You're just jealous, cuz I didn't get to you first." He pushed up out of the sofa's deep springs and kissed her on the cheek.

"Next time, Joan," he said, walking back into the kitchen with his shoulder blades cutting into the thin cloth of his T-shirt.

Daddy winked at Senator Russell—Ada. "Growing up to be a politician, I guess."

Ada looked around the room. "Either that or a whore."

"Isn't he in school?" I asked her.

Maury looked up from the cribbage game he was playing against himself. "Aren't you supposed to be in school? What about that, Sis?"

"Early graduation," Ada explained. "They ought to pass a law against it. I ought to pass a law."

Daddy picked at the sleeve of her robe, where the quilting was coming undone in little white tendrils. "After you get dressed, Senator."

"After my sons all leave home and it's too late to make any difference."

Joan stacked up her papers and reshuffled them, like she'd done with the tarot deck. "But what about humanitarianism, Ada? What about saving other people from their lazy sons?"

"Save it for law school," Maury said. "Here we just worry about our personal interest."

"Here? You mean here in Danitria?" Joan blew her hair away from her face, and I saw that she was sweating at the temples. But even sweat looked like jewelry on Joan.

"The Danitria of the soul," Daddy said.

"The Danitria of the mind," Maury told her.

"The Danitria of the body," I added, and everyone looked at me.

Ada stood up, adjusting her robe. "Get that girl a hobby before it's too late," she said, then disappeared down the back hall, her boots squawking like wounded birds.

I got up too and left Daddy fingering the label of the whiskey, Maury playing cribbage, Joan pouting. "I need to get some water," I told them, though no one seemed to be paying any attention.

In the kitchen, Tim sat cross-legged in a chair, drinking a beer and letting a gray hound dog, skinny as a model, lick at his other hand. Tim's thighs showed the same curved, sparse muscles as his dog's legs did. His scar was hidden, pressed against the plastic cushion of the chair, and I wondered if it would hurt when he stood up and the skin pulled away from the sticky surface. I had a scar in almost the same place on my leg, from the time Dot broke open her piggy bank and we danced a ring-around-the-rosy in the money and the glass. I wound up with sixteen stitches and Dot wound up with her own bank account. The scar still hurt sometimes too, when I wore short dresses in the cold, or when I was angry or bored.

I stood in the entranceway trying to think of an excuse for being there. Then I saw that Tim was talking to someone already, a boy leaning against the back door wearing a nylon basketball jersey and low-cut sneakers without socks. He had stubby brown hair the color of eraser nubs. I could tell his eyes were green and crazy from clear across the room.

"Hey, I know you," he said, and Tim turned around to look at me. My face changed from the inside out, and no matter how hard I tried to look blank, I knew I couldn't do it. That's why I knew the color of his eyes—I was remembering, not noticing. "Don't you know me, babe?"

"Russ, right?" I said.

He rolled his eyes at Tim and laughed. "Sometimes. But in this hick town it's Craig. Craig Russell."

"Your cousin?" I asked Tim. "Your brother?"

"Genetic accident," Russ said. "We're trying to get it fixed." He opened his mouth to laugh again, but the corners of his lips stuck together the way they had that night at the Governor's Ball. His mouth was pale and raw, and the upper lip had too many points to it, like the lip of a can opener.

"You never told me who you were related to," I said.

"You never told me your phone number."

"I thought you were the bartender."

"I thought you were a page. Some lucky bastard's page."

"They don't let in pages anyway. Not unless they're someone's date."

On the night of the Inaugural Ball, my father promised me I wouldn't have to sit out a single dance. I had on a silky maroon dress strapped over one shoulder and I looked like an Amazon or the Statue of Liberty. But Maury stayed in the bathroom too long picking up football tickets and making friends, so Daddy had to waltz with me himself. In person–no ambassadors. After three measures, we were already out of step, but he shuffled around even more and made a joke out of it. I picked a petal off his boutonniere and tucked it into my hair. He pulled out another one and dropped it on the floor. Petal by petal, we peeled his red carnation down to the stem. We did a corny turn that looked like it belonged in a square dance. Then he stopped. A woman had cut in on us. She wore a dress made out of fabric from a space suit, and hair cut to match.

"My turn, Mr. Right Honorable Martin," she said. "Listen dear," she told me, trellising her arm over his neck, "they've got disco dancing in the Frontier Room. Why don't you give that a whirl?"

I didn't want to watch them, and I didn't want to wait for Maury either, so I just went. The music rushed up and went through all my limbs. In here, the party had spilled off the dance floor. Girls stood on the tables and kicked over ice buckets. Behind the buffet, a man was doing a striptease, tossing his clothes up to catch the antler horns on the wall. A woman had her boyfriend backed up onto a barstool and she was shaking her garter at him.

The strobe lights spit into my eyes and the music stabbed up my legs, like the little mermaid when she stood on human feet. I needed to dance, just to feel at home in that room. I started alone, at the corner of the floor. Then a boy in a white tuxedo came up and danced with me. He didn't say a thing, only danced closer and closer, touching my hair and my arms and dress as he moved.

At a break in the music, he said: "I'm Russ. What's your phone number? What's your name? What's your favorite position?"

"I'm just here to dance, OK? They told me to come in here and dance."

He brought his face up close to mine and laughed, lolling his head around so it looked like it might fall off. His lips were gummy and pink; his eyes were green and full of wires.

"Oh, I get it," he said. "Now you run home at midnight and masturbate, right?"

vii

Ada decided to put us—the girls—in Russ's room, since he was the youngest and he had bunk beds and spent half his night on a sleeping bag on the back porch anyway. I wandered into the bedroom alone while the rest of them were still talking arrangements. It was dark, with rows of walnut paneling too close together and a dense smell of turpentine. That and the big, serious, unmatched furniture made it seem more like a den than a bedroom. Russ only had one picture in the whole room, a black-and-white cartoon cut out of a newspaper. It showed a man with a broad face and glasses counting money at a table with a frizzy-haired woman in cowboy boots that came up to her thighs. Her shirt was unbuttoned and a bill was sticking out of her bra. Behind them, the various senators were sitting in an amphitheater watching the governor fight a bull. "How are we doing, Moll?" the man who was supposed to be my father said. I'd never seen that one before.

I set my knapsack down on the lower bunk and wondered if Joan would let me sleep on top. Most adults would automatically say go ahead; they wouldn't even want to climb up on the ladder and look under the eaves for ghosts and spiders, then dream of falling all night. But Joan was different. She'd probably want to sleep up there just to prove she was lighthearted and unpretentious, despite all her family's money.

I changed my mind and dragged my knapsack off onto the floor. Which bed did Russ sleep in? And why did he have two? I didn't want to sleep in his room anyway, whether I got the bottom bunk or the top. It was like the time my grandfather died and they made me stay in his bed on the night before the funeral. They didn't think I knew he died in the big oak bed with the hammock sag in the middle and the smell of raw piecrust in the sheets. But I did. I knew and had to pretend I didn't because of how it would upset my grandmother if I brought up such a thing. So I stayed and had nightmares and threw up instead. I remembered about our grandfather always wanting us to sleep with him when we were little and how Dot went ahead but I wouldn't. I thought it was bad, or gross, or I just didn't want to be touched. I wondered if I wanted to feel guilty about it now, or if I should feel guilty, or if I did. I threw up again, and this time it was only water. My mother came in and held her cool, beautiful hand to my forehead. Like an ice sculpture at a wedding. My father went out to the 24-hour convenience store to buy me some soda. Then they stayed up with me all night.

But that was when they still did things together, before we had to take sides. I walked across Russ's room and set my knapsack down by the desk instead. It was a drafting table with the board pressed down flat. I turned on the green glass lamp and saw my hand glow red and gold. I thought I could even see the bones under my plump little finger pads, like the stone inside a cherry. That's what was really me, I thought—the stark, ungirlish part no one wanted to know about. Except maybe you did, and you decided the only way to do it was by cutting through to me. My arm shivered in the prickly heat from the lamp, and I reached under the desk for a drawer or map or key taped to the underside. All I found was a smooth surface with pits carved into it at intervals. I tried to read them, Braille-like, but I couldn't make out any letters. So I pulled out the straight-backed chair and crawled under the desk to look. No writing. But I smelled gum and grease and orange peels, found unused BBs and cigarette papers in the crack between the carpet and the baseboard.

"Libby," someone said from the doorway. "Libby, are you decent?"

It was Russ or Tim. The voice was tenor sax with bass notches in it. Like a white birch tree with black bands around its arms. Tim or Russ, I wondered. I guessed Russ. I didn't want to come out from under the desk. First because it was too embarrassing and then because I liked the room better from there.

I didn't answer and the person outside the door came in anyway.

"I'm not that ugly, am I?" he said. "What, did you see a rat, or one of Russ's iguanas maybe?"

So it was Tim. I backed out from under the desk and felt my skin shimmer everyplace my dress touched. My nylons made a cricket noise when I stood up.

"What iguanas? Where?"

He pointed to an aquarium on the bottom shelf of the stereo stand. Inside, a green lizard with the head of a dinosaur was draped over a piece of driftwood. Its fluorescent green skin didn't seem real, but more like new green moss growing thicker in the folds. There was another one too, hiding beneath the branch, its skin the same green mottled with spots of brown. Tim and I stood looking at them, and I could feel his hand fracture the air by my arm, even though he wasn't actually touching me. I shivered again, from the nape of my neck all the way to my ring finger.

"Do you really think they're ugly?" he asked, and then he did touch me, so definitely that I couldn't remember anymore what it felt like before he did it.

"They're not exactly ugly," I said. "They're more just evil-looking."

He nodded and lifted the hair away from my ear. "It's the tails. Otherwise, they'd look just like matchbook cars."

"The heads aren't so pretty either," I said, leaning away from his hand.

"They're OK. They're just complicated, with all those horns and things. Why is it people think simple is good and whatever's complicated is evil?"

I looked over at him and concentrated my face into its most adult shape. "I bet you heard that in school, huh?"

"I don't go to school, remember?"

"Then you read it in a book."

"Maybe a comic book," he said, and laughed.

"I have a boyfriend, you know."

"One in every precinct."

"At home."

"So, are you going to let me kiss you now?"

I couldn't believe he asked, just like that. If he hadn't asked, I would've let him. As it was, I picked up my knapsack and started unpacking it: curlers, toothpaste, shampoo.

"You're probably only trying to get secrets out of me," I said. I squeezed out a dab of toothpaste and set it on my tongue. Then I held out the tube to him.

"Thanks," he said, and set the tube on the desk behind him, then leaned down and licked the toothpaste off my tongue.

His mouth was warm and salty against the cold sting of the spearmint. I let him go on until the toothpaste flavor started to melt into spit and then I stepped away.

Tim bit his lip. "And that means it's your quota, I guess."

"I guess it is," I said. "I guess you can quote me on that."

Joan walked into the room without knocking and threw her overnight case onto the bottom bunk. The case was red, round, shaped like a hatbox, and she threw it so hard it rolled off the other side. Then she was gone again.

"Quite the lady, aren't we?" Tim said.

"Who? Joan or me?"

"Well, both. It looks like both, today. You'd probably do some wicked double-dating."

"Ha," I said, and Joan was back again. She had all the

papers, printouts, letters, notebooks, briefcases for the hearing and she began laying them out in separate piles on the floor. It looked like she was papering the whole room in political information. She sat down and husked off her heels, heel to toe, then went back to work.

"Hey, over here," Tim said. "You're backing us into a corner."

Joan looked up, running a hand along her silver hair, sharp and surgical in the artificial lighting of the room. "Sorry, I didn't see you there. Some of us are already cornered."

"What's wrong?" I asked, and stepped over the papers, flopping onto the bed on my stomach.

Tim followed me, picked up Joan's case and handed it to her, then sat down on my legs.

"Nothing," Joan said. "It's complicated."

I turned around to see Tim's smile, coming slowly, in jagged intervals, the way I knew it would. I felt myself smiling in the same rhythm and then wondered whose it was: his smile or mine?

"Your mother isn't too cooperative," Joan told Tim.

"Neither was my father. It's a family trait."

I felt him draw an imaginary line on my nylons, right where the scar would be on his leg. Then I wanted to look at his legs again. "What about you?" I said. "How cooperative are you?"

"The question is, do you really want to find out?"

"Hey, hey," Joan said, her chin bucking up. "No foreplay in the committee room."

"I thought it was the bedroom," Tim said. "It seemed appropriate to me."

"Do you just want us to get out of your way?" I asked her.

"No. No, I'm used to working in an atmosphere of heavy pheromones."

"Geez," said Tim. "You go to college and they teach you all these dirty words. That's why I quit school."

"It must be those keen moral values you grew up with," Joan told him. "Still, I don't see you pulling in the fundamentalist vote from your district."

"The fundamentalists are more interested in pulling out, if you know what I mean."

Joan laughed a diachronic scale, one step at a time, hesitating on the next to last stair. "I thought that was the Catholics," she said. "Libby, we'll get to Catholic sex ploys next week."

My stomach squirmed inside me, and I slid my legs away from Tim. Then I sat up and saw Russ standing in the hallway. He wedged his fingers between the hinges of the open door and rocked it back and forth. Never really smashing it, just barely pinching his fingers.

"Body Scrabble," he said. "Can I play?"

"Yes," Joan told him, without turning around. "You can get your body into your mother's study and find me some highlighter."

"Sorry, I don't do that stupid stud stuff. Why don't you get your errand boy Maury to run it over for you?"

Joan stopped for a moment and turned to us. "So where is Maury?"

Tim shrugged, his curls tugging up onto his shoulders. "I'll get it if you like."

"OK, but don't be thinking I owe you any favors."

Tim went out and Russ stood there swinging in the doorway for a while. He flexed his fingers, grasped the doorjamb on either side of him, reached up and pulled at the top of the doorframe.

"They're probably screwing. Right now," he said.

Joan kept on separating papers, only faster. I sat trying not to move, even though the muscles in my calves were strung as tight as catgut—bows and strings, bows and slings, bows and arrows that wanted to be released. If I didn't move, I wouldn't have to have a reaction at all. Everything would go on, and the word would float away as if it never happened. I remembered the first time I ever heard someone say it–screw. I was sitting in math class, going over my equations before the bell rang. Other people were still standing up, trading homework, inventing gossip, borrowing lies. A boy on one side of me called out to another boy over my shoulder: "Stud, did you screw her last night?"

"Yep," the boy said–Mark was his name. "Screwed her good and tight."

I reached underneath my knee and felt the round peg where the seat was bolted to the chair. Screw. The seat was bolted to the chair, the chair was bolted to the floor, and underneath, I knew, the world was moving. But I couldn't move.

The boys didn't look at me, but their faces turned lopsided in my direction. They went on talking about the girl. How she had a front-hook bra and leopardskin panties. How she didn't want to do it at first, but he–Mark Sanderson–got the keys to the concession stand where his brother worked and told her it would be good for her, it would probably make her tits grow. He finally got her legs spread on the counter under the snow cone machine. He bumped against it while they were fucking and ice and syrup slurped all over her, but that didn't slow him down any. How he licked snow cone off her pussy. How she was incredibly tight.

I was thirteen years old–so were they–and I hated them. Mark stood there with his hands in his jeans. He had on a white, blousy shirt that made him look full of wind and chest muscles and arrogance. I had a shirt just like that. I bought it to look like Mark Sanderson, who everybody loved and was afraid of and bought cigarettes and baseball tickets for. Sometimes, in bed at night, I pretended Mark Sanderson was in love with me. He put his hand around my waist and let it slide down over my hips, lifting my skirt a little, but never too high. He kissed my eyelids, my earlobes, even the moles under my hair. Then maybe I'd let him take off his shirt. But sometimes, even more secret, I pretended I was Mark Sanderson who was in love with me. Then, when he pushed his tongue like a squirming goldfish against my teeth, I didn't have to decide whether to open my mouth or not: we were both inside already.

Russ took one last swing on the doorframe, then came in and sat down beside me. "Did you ever see your parents screwing?" he said. "It's not like in the movies. They don't kiss around a lot. They just get right to the punch line."

Joan looked the way she did when she was listening to Republican speeches, like swallowing aspirin without water. "What makes you think all parents screw the same, just because they're parents? Everybody screws different, if you really want to know. Even the same people screw different with different partners."

"So, how do you know?"

"I'm psychic," Joan said. "Get out of here and leave Libby alone."

But then Tim was back with the highlighter and Maury was right behind him. Maury tossed me a frosted cupcake wrapped in cellophane; then he reached down and gave one to Joan.

"Good news, Judge. Larkin and Mills are both going to be there for you to push around."

"Oh, good. Isn't anybody worried about this except me?"

"What's to worry?" Maury said. "You're already in like Flynn up there at Harvard Law School."

"That's not what I meant." She tore into the cellophane with her long fingernails and picked the icing off the cupcake. That's all she ever ate, just the icing.

Rich people, I thought.

Then Daddy and Ada were in the doorway too, without ever walking up to it. That's how my grandfather used to appear to me after he died, ever since the night I threw up in his bed. I'd be coloring in front of the television set or dressing one of my dolls and he'd show up on the mantle or in the fireplace or in front of the sliding glass doors to the patio. Standing there with my grandmother like they were a pair of salt shakers—some of the tacky souvenirs he sold out of his truck. A shepherd and shepherdess. Hansel and Gretel. The King and Queen of Hearts. What I couldn't figure out was—what was my grandmother doing up there with him? She wasn't dead yet. She was still alive, wearing new pastel pantsuits and working in a wholesale business downstate. So I tried to pick her up and set her down outside the picture. But it never worked.

That's how I felt about Ada now. She didn't belong there, but no one seemed to think anything about it. It was up to me to set the picture straight. Ada had on a plain rust-colored dress with a matching blazer, but the way she stood there, it might as well have been a robe. She pushed down the graying fizzle of her curls and pulled an invisible hair out of her mouth. Daddy shuffled his eyes over the room, found Joan, then me, kept me focused while he patted down his coat pockets looking for something. Ada reached into her jacket and handed him a lighter. It was his—the tortoiseshell one he bought for himself when he was in high school—the one he had at my aunt's wedding.

When I saw that, I couldn't stay just sitting on the bed. I walked up between them and took the lighter from my father's hands. I'd never thought of him as strong before. Ma'am was the strong one. But now he seemed so proud and powerful that I had to take something away. It was disappointing, even, how easily he gave it to me. Because he must've thought I was just coming up to kiss him. He leaned toward me and I was looped into the cloud of his breath—a smell so rich and sour it turned up sweet again. I felt the rough rind of his cheek and the stubborn shape of his stomach. Then I opened his fingers, point by point. It was as simple as opening an orange.

"So Sly, you started smoking now?"

"No," I told him. "But maybe I'm going to." I picked up the stack of papers nearest me and flicked at the lighter. Two, three spins of the wheel and it still wouldn't flare, just shrieked dully along.

"Take it easy, Lib. We're about to ramble."

The flame engaged in a tang of sulphur.

"We won't need them anyway," I said. "It's the discard pile." I touched a two-page document to the flame, watching it curl into ash.

Daddy raised both eyebrows at Joan and she made the shape of "no" with her mouth. He moved toward me and Maury moved in from the opposite direction. But before they could get to me, I dropped the papers and ran out of the room, brushing against Ada's small, fat breasts, loose and jiggly as nervous gerbils under her blazer. I kept the lighter, though. I didn't want either of them to have it.

Maybe that's what happened to the rest of your letters, I thought. Maybe my father took his lighter and burned them. Maybe I was never going to see them at all.

viii

After I left the room, I couldn't think of anyplace to go. I couldn't just run away from home–I was already away from home. Almost as far as I could get. And my father was the one who'd helped me escape. Though there was something here that was oddly like our house, I thought, passing through the mixed-up living room and grabbing a handful of unshelled peanuts on my way out the door. Ada's was the underside of home, like the inside of the brocade vest Ma'am made me for the Christmas dance. When the maroon thread disappeared into the pattern, it showed up on the other side of the fabric. So that the picture on the inside was exactly the opposite of the one you saw when I was dressed up in my new outfit. Like in a mirror, or negative, reversed. That was Ada's. Two boys instead of two girls. A mother that was a real, rough divorcée instead of just a political widow. And in their family, it was the oldest kid whom everybody loved, who was funny and uninhibited and curly-headed. Whereas the younger one was rude, changeable, problematic, like me. "The Problem Child," Ma'am called me, after some dumb poem she learned in school.

We were the reverse of them, they were the reverse of us, and Daddy was the needle–sharp, silver, slippery–that pulled us all together. It hurt, like pins and needles of frostbite, to think of things that way. But I made myself think it anyway. Then I had to hate my father too. And then I had to hate myself.

I thought of going back into the house and locking myself in the bathroom, but that was too obvious. Or of wandering off into the woods, but that would scare me as much as it would him. I decided to get back into the car, since it was the only thing here that had any connection to us, our family. I could always drive it away, if I had to. Then Daddy would be sorry for making me cart him around all those times, even though I was too young.

I crashed into the front seat, locked all four doors, and sat there cracking peanut shells. Bits of shell poked into my gums and salt stung in the raw corners of my mouth, making me feel better about it all: now I had an excuse to cry. Sometimes, it took a little edge of pain to start me off, then I could cry for all the sentimental reasons in the world—starving kids in Africa, the invisible net of arguments between my parents, the boy who never called back after the prom. It was like what Daddy said to me when I was small: "Stop crying or I'll give you something to cry about." He thought it was logic—fear and pain and punishment—that made people cry, but even then I knew those things were only keyholes to see your sadness through. Let him spank me, I'd think. It couldn't make my life any worse anyway, and afterward I'd be able to stay in my room reading sad animal stories and crying all afternoon, then he'd feel even guiltier.

I finished the peanuts and started pulling the shells back out of the ashtray, one by one, and setting them on fire. The crossed strands of fiber took a long time to burn down. It smelled like burning rope. "I'm at the end of my rope," I said out loud to myself. It sounded like my mother. The stiff, high, crackly voice of church hymnals. I hated that voice, but I couldn't stop using it. All my life, I couldn't stop imitating people. I couldn't decide who I hated imitating most, my mother or my father.

A shell burned down to my fingertip and I held it for as long as I could, the pain bright and hypnotizing behind my eyes. I tried it with another shell. If I could just do this long enough, I was sure I'd never be scared or angry again.

Joan came out and knocked on the car window. She did

it in a prissy way that annoyed me, holding back her thin white wrist and showing off the fine veins that ran together like blue highways on the demographics map.

"What do you want?" I said, and rolled the window down.

"Your father's getting upset about you. Not a very good photo opportunity back there."

"Every now and then I have to slack off and act like a fifteen-year-old, OK? It's role-playing, you know? Anyway, why doesn't he come out here himself?"

She reached inside the window and unlocked the door. "You know why. He's scared."

"I know," I said. "But it's embarrassing. He ought to be embarrassed to be scared of his own kid."

"Scoot over, kid. You're his daughter. He's supposed to be scared of you. Don't you ever read any psychology?"

"That's not until senior year."

"Get a library card, Libby. You might need it before then."

She opened her purse and took out a black-and-red lacquered case with a dragon painted on it.

"I don't want to play with your makeup," I told her. "It's not going to make me feel any better. I'm too old for that now."

"But you're not too old for this," Joan said, opening the case and handing me a homemade cigarette rolled as tight as a toothpick and twisted at one end. "Besides, it'll make me feel better even if it doesn't help you."

She handed me the joint and I lit it, gave it back to her. The smell was everywhere already, laying itself down rich and thick as a layer of spice cake. Joan took a hit and held her breath in, her arms crossed in front of her and her lips pressed together tight.

"Now you try," she said, letting out the smoke in an impatient huff of incense.

"I don't get high."

"Well, don't worry. I'm not an informer for the government."

"No, I mean I can't. Michael keeps giving me stuff but nothing ever happens."

"Let's see. Michael. The boyfriend. You know, Libby, getting high is like getting an orgasm. You have to teach yourself how to do it. And it's easier when there aren't any men in the room."

I took the joint from her. "OK," I said. "But this never works. It's just a waste on me."

"Inhale. Inhale and think of Jack Kennedy."

"Why?"

"Or whoever."

I took a drag and the smoke grated along my throat. It was worse than gargling, and I let out the whole hit.

"You've got to hold it in. Really, it's worth it."

I tried again, and this time I managed to keep most of the smoke down for about half a minute.

"So, is my father actually sleeping with Senator Russell?"

Joan took off her shoes and slid her feet onto the dashboard. Her nylons had sheer toes, and underneath her toenails were short, straight, painted coral even before swimsuit weather. My toes would never look like that. "Well, Libby, what do you think?"

"I don't know. How do I know what adults do?"

She passed the joint again. "How do I know either?"

"You're like a spy," I said. "You're in-between."

"You mean like a double agent?"

"Sort of."

"I'm not sure if that's a compliment or an insult."

"You get to pick," I told her.

"Libby, a man like your father. A guy, really. You can't expect him to be like other fathers. He's better and he's worse. My father, for one, would never drag me around like Tom does you. But he wouldn't pay attention to me either. He just bought me skating lessons and trampolines and things."

"That's like Daddy, though. He just sends you out to talk to me instead."

Joan pinched the joint tighter and took another hit. "It's not the same thing."

"It is so," I said. Something skipped inside my head. It was like using a gearshift. My whole mind pushed up against my forehead, cold and impatient. "Hey, I think I did it. I think I'm high."

"Well, how is it?"

"It's like–what's that blue stuff you keep in an ice pack in the freezer?"

"Freon?"

"Freon. It's like having Freon in your brain."

She laughed. "I told you it was worth it."

"Except it doesn't make me feel any better," I said, laughing with her.

"Uh-huh. I can see you're all broken up."

"I am," I said, then I started to cry again. But I couldn't stop laughing at the same time. I laughed. I coughed. I sputtered. Like a stream choked in its own pebbles.

Joan reached over and kissed the top of my head. "Rain and sunshine, Sunshine," she said. "The devil's beating his wife."

Yes, I thought, but who's the devil and who's the wife. "And even worse," I told her, "I've got my period and I don't have anything for it and I'm not about to ask that senator."

She checked her purse. "Here, I always carry one with me, like a cyanide capsule. Just in case."

It was a tampon in a white wrapper with blue writing on the side.

"I don't know how to use these," I said.

"Read the directions. Figure it out. Then we can all go swimming later. Otherwise, you'll just be sitting out on the sidelines."

"Well, I'll try. Give me another one, just in case I mess this one up."

"I'll tell Tom you're on your way, all right?"

"Sure," I said. "Tell him whatever you want."

She jostled my knee and gave it a little pinch, then went back into the house, carrying her purse flat and important against her chest, like she was still in high school.

I looked at the wrapper. "Grasp cord and pull," was all it said. Peeling it open, I found a thin string, like the wick of a candle, and two cardboard tubes, one inside the other. One was packed with cotton and the other was hollow. I knew the cotton part went inside, with the string hanging down. But it seemed like too much to fit inside me all at once. Besides, the cardboard was hard, with sharp edges. I slid the smaller tube around inside the bigger one. I didn't want to do it; I didn't have permission to do it. But now I'd told Joan I would and she'd know I'd backed out if I didn't go swimming. So I had to try.

Though not in Ada's house with all those boys hanging around. If I had to do it, I'd rather just stay out here.

I looked around, then out the rearview mirror. The neighborhood seemed empty, and I'd never had much modesty anyway. Dot and I changed clothes in the car all the time, sliding down the backseat to take our shirts off and racing to see who could get dressed again the fastest. I never felt my body was something to be proud or ashamed of, either one. Until one day, I was around ten, and we were dressed up for church in white eyelet dresses. Dot's had pink flowers on it, mine had blue, with ribbons and sashes to match. We were playing surfers in the living room, sliding across the polished wooden floor in our socks. Daddy was asleep–half asleep–on the sofa, and Ma'am came through the room with a coffee cup and a can of hairspray. "OK, girls," she said. "Can't you learn to wear a slip or at least an undershirt? People look at you and they can see those little brown spots right through your dresses." In front of my father, who pretended to be asleep. But I knew he wasn't. His breath was too tricky and irregular under his open tuxedo shirt. His eyelashes fluttered; his throat muscles yawned, even though he never opened his mouth.

I wanted to take the hairspray away from my mother and spray it in her face. I wanted to turn into a sea monster. I wanted to rip off my eyelet dress and never wear any clothes again. I wanted–I'm sure I thought this–to take a magic marker and color my nipples blue.

But I started wearing a slip anyway. And about the same time, I started taking my shirt off in the vacant lot when we played Indians and running out in my nightgown to get the mail. I looked out the rearview mirror again. A little boy on a bicycle steered into my blind spot, then veered off in the other direction. No one else. I lifted myself off the seat and pulled my pantyhose down halfway to my knees. Underwear too. The bloody toilet paper fell out and I threw it in the ashtray, touched the lighter to it, burned it away until it dissolved into the general smell of pot and perfume. Then I dropped the lighter, took a breath, thought of how I hated my mother, and pushed the cardboard up inside me. It hurt, the edges pinching at the opening, and I had to work it in. Tight. So tight I felt plugged up and almost suffocated before I noticed I wasn't breathing and had to remind myself: inhale, exhale, think of Jack Kennedy, and repeat. Sit straight, keep your legs together, don't talk about your teachers that way–I have to see them at the school board meeting. Is there going to be pot at that party? If there is, you better not go. It doesn't matter to the police whether you partake or not; to the police it's all the same. And then you'll land yourself and your father on the front page of that filthy rag this town calls a newspaper. Tell Michael you can't just sit out there in the car all night. People are driving past this house at all hours, any hour. Your father stays out all hours, comes in at any hour, you sit there talking on the phone for two hours, and I was up cleaning the house hours before you even woke up. I'll give you one hour, down there in the basement with Michael, then I expect you to make him go home.

I contracted the muscles inside me, then expanded them.

Sixty times would be a minute, sixty minutes would be an hour. For Ma'am, everything ran straight like that, until she couldn't stand it anymore and she flew off the clock in a rage. But with Daddy, time lapped like a dog from a dish. Like Ada's dog. So with him, I never knew how much longer I had.

I adjusted the cardboard again, and made sure I could find the cord in its slick nest, as if I were something that could explode. "What time is it?" Michael would say, when he'd gotten me down to my bra and underwear. I think he was trying to break his own record. He used to tell me I was frigid, that I couldn't understand how a guy felt. But I was always hearing the minutes tick behind my eyelids, in my armpits, on the backs of my knees. The minutes in the basement and the minutes before I could leave home and the minutes of my life.

Still, Ma'am told me: "There's no difference–don't let him get away with that. What you feel is just as intense as what he feels. He's just prouder of feeling it, that's all."

And I believed her. At least, I wanted to believe her. But how did she explain about my father and Ada then? Did she feel the same as him? Then why didn't she have a real lover instead of the imaginary guys I made up for her? I pulled up my underwear and inched the nylons back up my legs, then rearranged my dress around my knees.

There was a noise from the garage and I touched my foot to the brake in reaction. Someone was in there. The noise came again, in a jangle of metal, and Russ trudged out onto the grass with a lawn chair, sat down, and started cutting up the hem of his jeans. He stopped just below the knee, then stood up and grasped at the ripped leg with both hands, his body gripped and shaking. The sun licked up the red in his hair. I crushed the cardboard tube in my hand and the denim finally gave. Russ straightened up again, his face raw from straining. He didn't cut the jeans any higher, or work on the other leg. Instead, he sat down, opened the tackle box, and picked out lures, testing their sharpness against his finger, and laid them out carefully on his knee. Then he started hooking them to the ripped-up pant leg hanging to his right thigh in shreds. He put in about five hooks, looked up and stared right into the car window. Made a circular motion with his hand.

And I rolled the window down.

"Libby, babe. How about an earring?" He held up an orange-and-purple lure with long legs and antennae, a huge sharp hook on the end.

"Come here," I said.

"What?"

"Come over here and bring it to me."

"You like that, huh?"

"At least it's interesting, anyway."

He stood up and dropped the garden shears to the lawn, but kept the tackle box under his arm. As he came closer, his face got redder and more real, so that it hurt to look at him. His short nose had a flat spot on the end, as if he were pressed up against an invisible window. One pimple on the forehead, one on the chin, both spread out like anthills. Green eyes with a thousand brown scratches across them.

"Here, chickie," he said, when he got up by the front window. "Want me to stick it in for you?"

"Why don't you get in first?"

"In that slimy, state-sponsored bossmobile?"

"Yep," I said. "Right here."

He walked around, opened the door, and scooted toward me, too close.

"Give it here," I told him, then I took out my earring and put the fishhook in instead, twisting the wire together at the back so it wouldn't cut me.

I handed him the earring, an opal on a silver backing like an old-fashioned teaspoon. "Here, for luck." Then I started the engine.

"Luck. A guy like me doesn't need bad luck. I eat it for

breakfast. I shit bad luck. I'm used to it. I don't even want to be lucky anymore. What do I need to be lucky for?"

"Because I'm kidnapping you," I said, and backed out of the driveway without looking behind me.

ix

You didn't know that about me: I can scare people too. It just takes me longer, is all. Dot and I used to have a political prisoner game where we'd catch someone—it had to be a boy—and chain him to the black doghouse behind the swing set in our backyard. Daddy built that house from scratch back before he got to be a senator and he was hanging around home all the time with nothing to do. But our dog, Chief, would never go in there, and we had to give him away to some family in the country after he ran off the third time and Ma'am found him checked into the lobby of a motel, lying under the front desk eating a dead robin. So we felt responsible, really, to try to find something to do with Chief's property.

Here's the plan, I'd tell Dot: get a butterfly net, then chase someone, hopefully a bully, around the neighborhood until he's exhausted and has to come home with us. Take away his clothes. Chain him to the doghouse. Force-feed him mushes made of long, rainy-day worms and box-elder bugs and moldy mulberry leaves. Poke a rose thorn in his finger and make him write a ransom note in his own blood. Prick his finger again and drip some blood sauce on his dinner. Play kickball on the lawn in front of him, but never let him up to kick. Make him miss a whole grade of school, so he has to go back and do it over again. Shoot marbles with him, then cheat and don't admit it. Rub iodine over his skin. Peel his scabs. Pluck his eyebrows. Bite his tongue.

Whenever I thought about it, my mouth tasted of the wild rhubarb that grew at the side of our house.

But there weren't any bullies in our neighborhood. Only

little boys who hadn't started losing their baby teeth yet, chunky girls in playsuits with ruffled bloomers, tomboys who were always climbing trees or playing horses and never walked on two feet.

We finally tried our game out on Maury's nephew, when Maury was on the rich side of town putting up yard signs with our father.

"We're babysitting you now," I told him. "So you have to do what we say."

He pointed his Star Trek laser gun at my ear. "Correction. I'm older. I devise the bylaws."

"Not in warp speed," Dot said. "Or Vulcan years or whatever."

Maury's nephew picked at his scalp and rolled his eyes. "Holy cow pie, you're never going to get the galactic system straight."

I took his gun, like I was interested in how it worked, then stuffed it nose down between the sofa cushions. "You're right. We'd just mess it up. Why don't you humor us and just play our game with us instead?"

He reached down for his gun and put it back in a special pocket of his Army jacket. "What do I have to do?"

I sat out at the doghouse with him while Dot made her own version of mud pie. He let me tie the chain in a loose bracelet around his wrist and he took off his pants when I told him to, but insisted on keeping his jacket. His legs were the grimy white of cooked oatmeal, and they were peeling on the thighs and ankles. He pulled off a long white scab and held it out to me. Three blond hairs stuck to it.

"Glue," he said. "Fake scabs. I construct these when I'm bored, mostly, or when I'm watching TV."

"Geez. Are you trying to wax your legs or something?"

"What?"

The guy had a genius IQ, but he didn't know what leg wax was. "Never mind. I guess I'm supposed to torture you now."

He wrinkled his forehead into fat ridges. "What technique are you going to use?"

I looked around. A yellow plastic bucket filled with rainwater. Some Martin signs leaning against a tree. A rake. A rusted trowel. A stalk of purple thistles.

"Nettles," I said. "Nettles in your nose and under your fingernails."

He pulled his legs up to his chest. They were more purple than white now, and goose bumps were rising around the patches of glue, pulling them tight. "That's unnecessarily primitive, don't you think?"

I pushed the trowel in around the thistle plant so I wouldn't have to touch the leaves. "Well, you get used to it. That's how we do things here on earth."

Then I set a row of nettles on my sleeve, like cuff buttons. "Pull your legs up. I want to get closer."

I knelt in front of him and held his face up to me, thought about the plastic skulls Maury hung up on our porch the Halloween before when he chaperoned our party. By the end of the night, Dot figured out how to drink orange sherbet punch out of them, and she had everyone copying her. I could drink out of this boy's skull, I thought. I could suck up his eyes and sip spit out of his mouth. His body shifted; maybe he could tell what I was thinking. He smelled bad, like a stew made out of meat no one bought in a grocery store. Venison. Daddy brought some home once and only Ma'am would try any. Dot felt guilty, so she slipped pieces in her milk and didn't get caught until later, when everyone thought it was funny. But I got up and fed mine to Chief, right in front of everyone. "I'm not eating dogmeat," I said. "No matter what kind of stories you make up about it." Afterward, when they sent me to my room to sulk in private, I tasted venison, rough and deep as a salt lick on the sides of my tongue. But I couldn't figure out how I remembered a taste I'd never tasted.

I looked back down at Maury's nephew and touched the

pink rim under his nostrils, where the cartilage rose up like another pair of lips. I pinched his nose open, pulled a nettle off my sleeve. He jerked from the chest out, the way Dot did when she dreamed of headless horsemen in the night, and I put the nettle up next to his nose, pressed it in, then pulled it out and kissed him. I cried and kissed him again, then licked up by his nose to take away the sting. But he tasted of sour cream potato chips and deodorant soap—not venison, not rhubarb, not the flavors at the edge of the tongue that I wanted.

Maury's nephew never said anything.

I ran into the house to have a fight with Dot over the wormy pie she was making and would never get to use.

"He fainted," I told her. "We'd be breaking the Geneva code if we did it now."

"Yellow belly fudge face. It was your idea."

"Well, we did it, didn't we?"

"I didn't get to do my part. Here, you eat this if you aren't going to make him do it."

When Daddy got home, Maury's nephew was sitting in the garage with his pants back on whittling lasers out of the signposts and Dot and I were wrestling on the kitchen floor.

I got grounded for two weeks, then paroled three days early to go to the cocktail party the Thorntons were throwing for my father. But once I got there, I went right into the back kitchen with Billy Thornton and vaporized a whole bottle of bourbon in a frying pan just so we could inhale the fumes and pretend to be drunk and stick our fingers in each others' clothes.

I told Dot that boys spit up blood when they did it. I told her I knew, because I did it with Billy Thornton.

I found an old rowing machine in a junk store and made my father buy it for me. Then I got my friends to come over and do exercises to make their breasts grow. They had to take off their shirts to make it work, and I'd lie on the bottom of the boat and watch their little nipples sharpen up like pencil nibs. I didn't want my breasts to grow.

I turned twelve.

I went to junior high.

I started my period.

Then Daddy got elected and I met Joan, who pinched my shoulders and asked why she didn't feel little bra straps there. During a Health, Education, and Welfare meeting, she took me shopping for a training bra with pads like the thick matting inside a bedspread and a lace butterfly with its wings spread open between double-A cups. For three months, I kept it hidden from my mother and only wore it in gym, or when Dot and I were playing cabaret dancers.

I got a new best friend, Réné, and when I spent the night at her house, she fed me Pepsi Light with lemon juice and Chex snack mix and asked me if I'd ever let anyone touch my breasts before I was married. She never would, she said. It was like drugs, you just did one thing and you could never stop. We could make a pact, she said, that we'd never let anyone do that. I said I wasn't so sure, I'd have to think about it, and then she fell asleep and I tucked the blanket between my legs and rubbed against the silky ribbon while I listened to her breathe.

I let a boy I didn't know pinch the cheeks of my ass together every other day when we lined up for study hall.

I found Michael's jacket lying on a piano bench in the music room and cut a sliver out of the seam with my nail clippers. Then I sprinkled it with leg and underarm hairs from my Daisy Wheel razor, wrapped it in an old nylon slip, and buried it in the violets beneath my bedroom window.

Dot and I wrote an anonymous love note to Eric, the boy from our church. We painted the number of our private phone line on the bottom of the page in nail polish. But he didn't call; his mother did. And we said it was the wrong number and hung up the phone.

Michael finally asked me out and I let him touch everything but my breasts, which I saved for last, until after I was sure that he loved me.

I burned my neck with a curling iron and told him it was a hickey.

I smelled my underwear when I got home from dates.

I sucked my opal ring.

I let the ruffles on my bedspread ride up between my legs while I was lying on my bed reading.

Then I grew up and kidnapped a rapist.

He was sitting next to me going through my father's glove compartment. "Hey, you got any hooch in here? Smells like you've got some hooch."

"Get away from there. I'm kidnapping you."

"Can't we get high while we do it, babe?"

"I'm already high and you're weird enough as it is."

He looked smaller over there in the passenger seat where Daddy usually sat. He had one knee pressed against the door and the other propped up on the seat so he could finger the shreds of his jeans. Drawing them out as long as they'd go, then scrunching them up again. Like he was playing with a girl's hair.

I turned down Fairfax Lane, away from the courthouse.

"This kidnapping deal, what's it into?" he said.

I stopped at a yield sign and looked at him, felt my jaw-bone turn solid again, after all the headless haze of marijuana. "You, Craig Russell Russ. It's into you, OK?"

"You aren't going to cut my ear off, are you? Then send it home in a bloody cocktail napkin? The kind with dirty jokes on it? Give old Ader a nice cheap thrill."

"I'm thinking about it. Where do you get lost in this town?"

"To the video arcade to get lost. To the Baptist church to get saved. That's pretty much it around here."

I pulled into the parking lot at a convenience store called Polly's Pantry—they didn't even have chains this far out in the sticks. "But where do you really go?"

He cocked his finger and flicked a tassel of his jeans at me, then looked up so fast his eyes were way ahead of the rest of his face. They were spooky enough, those eyes, like the changing show at a planetarium. "So why would I tell you?"

"I'll buy you a beer," I said, and pulled my father's money out of my wallet.

"Keep the fin," he told me, handing back my five and edging two singles into his hip pocket.

Count on a rapist to pay his own way.

While he was in the store, I grabbed a state road map out of the backseat and found Danitria. It didn't even get a whole circle, just a black dot like a flyspeck exactly between the capital and the state line. I didn't know which way was north, or how to find the highways from the main drive. Daddy only taught me how to steer; he never showed me how to figure directions. Sometimes I thought he didn't know how to do it himself, since he had Maury or Joan navigating most of the time.

Russ opened the door and heaved in a six-pack of a brand of beer I didn't recognize. Without a paper bag. He sat down, closed the door, put two fingers in his mouth and pulled out a plastic bubble of lip gloss. Wine color. In a lip-shaped case.

"For the outlaw lady," he said. "You know, if it's a Bonnie-and-Clyde gig you're going for. You're going to need a little more sleaze to carry it off."

"Carry you off, you mean. There's spit on it."

"Sorry, can't help drooling when I'm around you. The better to eat you with, my dear."

"Why was it in your mouth like that? Some new sort of high?"

"I don't know about that. But hey, we could try it. Why don't you put some on?" He opened the case, smudged some lip gloss on his finger, and tried to smear it on my mouth. But when I turned my head, he gave up, and spread it on his wrist in a messy, figure-eight doodle.

I started the engine. "Shoplifting. You probably had it in your mouth just so you could sneak it out of there."

Russ opened his beer with a violent slurp of metal that made me jump. "Not bad. They got you in police training class now?"

"No. Just the regular cocktail circuit."

He handed a beer toward me, but I ignored it. Then he pressed the cold can into my side, so I just took it and set it on the floorboard with the rest of the junk.

"Do you know where we're going?" I said.

"Canada? Las Vegas? Camino Real?"

I pressed my lips together, like Joan or my mother, and didn't say anything.

"OK, turn right," he said. "And drive straight till you get to the next hitching post."

We wound up on a dirt road with grass growing between the tire tracks. The deep ditches along the sides were filled with cow flowers, milkweed and black-eyed Susans. On the right was a barbed-wire fence and on the left a wall of trees and bushes.

I played my foot on the accelerator and sucked on my tongue. This was the kind of place we explored in Girl Scouts and told spook stories about. Escaped convicts. Severed heads. Bloody hooks. Nothing as bad as your letter, though. We couldn't even imagine yet what was in that letter.

"Well, babe. Are you stopping or not?"

I parked the car and looked around for a weapon. Fishing tackle. Rolodex. Blow-dryer. Then I remembered the golf clubs in the trunk. My father's mess of a life was good for something, anyhow. I went around to the back of the car and Russ followed me, touching my waist and shoulders as lightly as a phantom fever in the middle of July.

"No way. I don't do the trunk scene," he said. "They locked me in the closet too many times for that."

110

I opened the trunk and hunted around for the strongest iron. Then I changed my mind. I remembered a fairy tale I once heard on a record at school–the dark, spooky one that scared Dot so much I had to sleep in her bed with her for six months after I came home and told the story. In this version, the wicked stepmother lets the boy pick an apple out of an old, iron trunk. Then when he reaches in, she drops the lid down on his head, so it's rolling around inside with the other bad apples. The story goes on from there, but I always thought the trunk was the worst part– it sounded so much like something that could actually happen.

"Wait. You choose," I said.

"Choose what?"

"The club you want me to hit you with if you get out of line."

He brought his hand up to my face and I concentrated on not blinking. His fingers moved up to my eye. Then I really had to blink while he played around in the lashes and all I let myself think about was the smell of sweet grass and turpentine.

"Hold still. There's some sleep sand in your eye."

"Are you choosing?"

"I'm choosing. But you know I don't get out of line. That's because I never queue up in the first fucking place."

He leaned into the trunk and I saw his white scalp glisten where his hair parted in two different places, as if he couldn't make up his mind. Pearly paths like the tracks a snail makes on a rock. The spring on my father's trunk was broken. That meant all I had to do was let go and it would drop down on Russ with sixty pounds of pressure. But what would you kidnap someone for, if you were just going to kill them right away like that? You'd get something out of them first, right? Fear or sweat or lust or information? I loosened my hold a little, let the weight of the lid drag on my hands.

Then I felt a tug at my belt. Russ was twisted around in the trunk some way, lying on his back on the golf clubs. He'd have to be double-jointed, I thought, to flip over into a position like that.

He pulled my belt tighter, so my whole body curved with the tension, my chest tilted toward him and my hips planted behind me, keeping my balance.

"Guess I caught you with your hands full, babe. Gee, my favorite position." Reining in my belt, he reached for my breast. But I swerved away. Then he moved in again, and this time he caught my breast and pinched it, clamped it tight in a fist we were both part of.

My voice grated in my throat without making a sound. A fast, electric pressure glided up my arms like the slide of a trombone and made me shiver. I wanted to make my nipple as hard as his hand. I imagined it so sharp it pierced a hole in his palm. Holes in his hands like Jesus, nailed to the tree. "Sometimes it causes me to tremble," we used to sing. "Were you there when they nailed him to the tree?" "Nailed" was what they said about girls too. Once at the pool, two guys were sitting at the lifeguard station talking about me. "Flat as a board," they said. "And never been nailed." I wasn't so flat now. Now one of us was getting nailed.

I clenched my teeth.

I coiled up my gut muscles.

I let go of the trunk lid.

And he caught it with his knees.

X

So I didn't kill him, even though I tried.

Before I could think what came next, the trunk was closed and his fingers were clamped into the tops of my arms. I grabbed his arms too and pushed back at him, but that only spun me around in a half-circle. Then he had me backed up against the car. The bumper was warm on the backs of my legs. He grabbed my waist and pushed me up on top of the hood, so that the license plate scraped against my nylons and made a shrieking sound. My ass rode up over the lock, the ornamental racing blade, and it felt like cement burns from falling on the playground when I was a very little kid. I think that's when I started to cry. The car dented in and dimpled with our weight, made a curved noise like a question. Cut off short. And then sounded again. His leg was between mine, scrolling my dress up around my hips, pinching just a bite of my thigh between his bare knee and the hood of the car. It was the leg with the torn-up tassels; they lay against my leg and tickled in the middle of all that, a vicious tickle, like a swollen mosquito bite that I couldn't scratch. He smelled of sweet baby vomit. I thought I was going to vomit. My stomach swirled up into a tight ribbon of nausea, the way ribbons on Christmas packages curled up when Ma'am shirred them with the open blade of the scissors. He moved his hands to hold my arms down. By then, my head was up against the glass of the front window, and when I tried to move, my hair caught in the windshield wipers. He pulled the loose strands away and pushed me up higher onto the glass, where I got my leverage and strained my whole body against his. I still couldn't move, but he wasn't coming any closer.

"What are you doing?" I said.

"I thought you like it rough."

"What are you doing?"

He didn't answer, but his hold loosened a little, like he was considering.

"Do you hate me because of my father?"

"I don't hate you, Libby babe. This is what people do. It's what they're all wheeling and dealing about, didn't you know that?"

"No," I said, wedging my foot out from under him. "Who?"

He felt it, hooked his foot around my leg, and pinned me back again. "You know, sweetheart, don't pretend to be a fucking virgin with me."

"But I am," I said. My face was wet with crying, only I had to keep it out of my throat. I was sure that would be the thing to make him attack me again, just the slightest vibrato of courage in my voice. "I am. But that doesn't make me stupid."

"Then why do you act like it?" he said, playing with a button of my dress, plying it back and forth like it was a loose tooth.

"Because there's just some stuff I don't know."

He unbuttoned the button. "Like what?" His fingers were warm against my sternum, then down to where my skin stretched tight over the windows of my ribs. I tensed my stomach, stopped. That was going to make me throw up for sure.

"Like about my father and Ada."

"Why don't you just let me show you instead?"

"Wait," I said. "And tell me first."

"Hey, OK, you want to be savvy, I'll trade you for it. Tit for tat. You give me a little titty and I'll tattle everything I know."

"You're not lying, are you?"

"Try me," he said, and unbuttoned another button.

114

I tried to look at him, to read his expression, but the sun was too bright and all I saw were silver camera flashes in slivers at the edges of my eyes.

"How did they start?" I said.

"He comes over one day last winter. It's bird season, right, and he wants to shoot pheasant. Or that's what he says, anyway. But shit, he didn't even bring his gun. So Ada gives him mine and they stay out all night. Then the next day I come home from school and there's Tom Martin in my kitchen, making pheasant with this queer sour cream sauce that smells like stale cum in a kleenex."

Button three was at my waist, and it gave with just a little extra pressure. Now Russ had his whole hand inside my dress, but he wasn't touching my breasts. In fact, my top two buttons were still fastened. He stroked my stomach, traced the lines of my ribs like he was studying to rebuild my skeleton from scratch, the way we did in sixth grade with boiled chicken bones. Michael had never done such a thing, and that made it seem worse, more creepy and perverted. "So he cooked for her. So what?" But I was thinking about how Daddy never cooked at home: I didn't even know the smell of the sauce Russ was talking about.

"So he hangs around for the next two days drinking whiskey and making phone calls. That Indian guy Tim works for keeps dropping by with fish or venison steaks or some plastic camping gear. Then he and Tom and Ada sit around yelling at each other. Tom just keeps making phone calls in between. Messing up the kitchen. And he eats, like, a whole slab of cheese out of the refrigerator, like it's an ice cream bar. Ada doesn't even bother to get dressed. She just wears that old tuxedo shirt and fuzzy orange socks everywhere she goes. They come in the kitchen and make pancakes and drink another shot of whiskey, then look at each other and go back upstairs. No one asks if I want any fucking breakfast, lunch, or dinner. No one remembers if it's breakfast or dinner. Tim took the car on a road trip over to Cartersville and Ada never noticed. I started letting the dogs sleep back on the sunporch and I'd bring down my sleeping bag and stay with them."

He seemed to forget about taking off my clothes. He just kept brushing my ribs in a heavy rhythm, like he was trying to hypnotize me.

"Then the third day Cyril shows up with Joan, who's carrying a suitcase. She says since the senators missed their meeting, they decided to have a makeup session here. Your dad says he'll get back to that next week, when more of the players will be in place anyway. But then she slides him a look like a trump card and he says OK, then let's get it over with. So she pulls out a bottle of Black Label and sets it in the middle of the table. Then comes the whole spread—cold cuts, bread, olives, cheese, out of a deli bag."

He was edging one finger under the elastic of my bra, not pressing, just exploring.

"And that's when she does the really kinky thing. She goes into the bathroom and changes into her nightgown. I know because I follow her down the hall, making out like I'm disgusted and I'm just going to go hang in my room. She doesn't even bother to close the door completely. So I see everything she's got. These tiny little tits with Band-Aids over them and a bush that's solid gold. Then she takes the Band-Aids off, real slow, and you can see it's hurting her and you can tell she doesn't mind."

Now I could feel him growing down by my leg, the way Michael did when we were making out in the basement. With Michael, though, I always tried not to notice. It seemed so rude to notice something about a person that they couldn't help. Michael told me if he held his breath he could stop it, like hiccups, and sometimes he did, for ten minutes or so, just to prove it was really true. Still, I wouldn't want to be that way, where people can see something that private about you without knowing you at all.

"And?" I said. "What happened after that?"

He moved his hand down to rearrange himself, or maybe just to make sure he was still there. "Then she goes in and sits down in the living room in this black nightgown with no underwear. I'm out there already, making myself a sandwich, since I haven't had anything but cold cereal and venison for two days. But no one else is eating. They all just look at Joan. Cyril tries to give your dad a cigarette, but he won't take it. He only bites his thumbnail and makes some serious progress on the Black Label. But the best is Ada. She starts cracking pecans and asks Joan if she wants to go to bed already, or if she's just modeling her trousseau. 'Trust me,' she said. 'You won't need that. They get bored with the frillies pretty quick. Then it's just you and your bones. How hot you can get their ass, how often, and how much faster than the competition.'"

"She said that in front of you?"

"I've heard worse," he told me. "Haven't you?"

"My father never talks dirty. He hates it when people say stuff like that."

"Yeah, well you can see how much he hates Ada." He undid the top two buttons of my dress. "Libby. Baby. Cunt muffin."

I bit the inside of my mouth to keep from screaming. "Are you going to tell me the rest of it or what?"

"What," he said. "You have to keep your bargain first."

He rolled all the way on top of me and the car dented in again. My ribs were squashed by his weight and I imagined them breaking up and poking into my heart and lungs in sharp little pieces. I could've killed him, I thought. I should've killed him, but then I'd never know the story.

He poked his fat, filmy tongue into my mouth, but I wouldn't open my teeth. He tried squirming his way in anyway until I finally just opened up and bit him. I tasted something runny and salty–blood or vomit–and when he let go of me to see what happened, I scooted off the car. If I could get into the front seat and lock all the doors, I could drive off, leave Russ and Ada and my father and never have to deal with them again. But Russ got to me first.

He grabbed me and wrestled me down until we were rolling around on the packed dirt and gravel of the road. This was better than on the car. I could use my legs down here, and I almost felt like I was winning at times. His hold would weaken, waver, and finally give. But that was only because he was getting ready to grip me in a new place. My dress was half off me, but I didn't care. It was only in my way. The gravel prickled my back and arms and stuck to my damp skin like the coating on fried chicken.

"Come on," Russ said. "You're not going to beat me. So what do you say, lady? Do you give? I can be real gentle if you just spread your legs and say please."

"Wait a minute." I knew if I hurt him in the right place, I could stop him, like turning off a machine. I reached down to one side of his fly, where I thought it would be. "What about you?" I said. "Do you have to say please?" And then my hand was wet, my leg too. At first I thought it was me– that I was so scared I wet my pants or my tampon had soaked through. But no, it was definitely Russ. There was a dark patch all over the front of his jeans. I remember Joan asked me once if Michael came off when we were playing around and I didn't know what she meant. She said, "Does he spout up on you, silly?" But that never happened with Michael before.

Russ didn't move. He was still holding onto me, only in a loose way that I could've gotten out of easy. The air smelled of egg salad sandwiches, and I remembered that's what I always wanted when it was a hot day and I'd been swimming for a long time. My arms ached. I put my finger through a run in my hose and felt through to my skin, which was ripped up in the same design.

"Well, I guess you're happy now," he said.

"Why?"

"Bitch. You're as bad as a grown one."

"So, are you going to tell me the rest?"

He pulled away from me. "Not until you earn it. Let's go get washed off."

I thought of getting into the car again and driving away, but there didn't seem to be much point anymore. So I followed Russ to the side of the road, where he scrunched down on his stomach and slid under the barbed wire. "Come on. Hurry up. I'm sticking to myself over here."

I touched the barbed wire once, twice, and pricked my finger.

"Here, I'll hold it for you," he said, and I crawled through. He could've gotten back at me then, but I knew he wouldn't. It was too late.

When I stood up again, I noticed I was walking wrong, funny, stilted. One leg seemed longer than the other and my knee felt magnetized–unsprung–like when the wire pops out of a fleshy plastic Barbie doll leg. But I could keep up with Russ anyway. I followed him through a field of stunted alfalfa and into a screen of trees. On the other side was a pond, still and round as a skating rink. A tin toolshed corrugated like a pie plate. An abandoned tractor seat.

"Where are we?" I said.

"Middle America. A farmer's field. Don't you read your state propaganda? No, this belongs to that Cyril guy Tim's working for."

"Yeah?"

"Yeah, he's building an ark."

"How come?"

He shrugged. "You've got to do something, even in a drought. Anyway, your daddy's pretty interested in it, whatever it is. Probably turns out, he's a drug lord or something." He yawned with his whole body and stretched off his shirt. "Are you coming in?" When he was stripped down to his underwear, I saw that his body wasn't ugly, only hard and skinny: flat in the muscley parts, bumpy where I expected a breathing space.

I poked my finger into the run in my nylons and pulled them apart. Then I walked into the water, dress and all.

Russ pushed in head first, then came up again shaking water off his hair in long silver arcs as regular as a sprinkler.

The pond water was warmer than the air outside. It lapped at my legs and seeped into the scraped parts of my skin, but didn't necessarily hurt. It pushed under my dress and lifted the skirt in a train. And I felt like the current was moving us, even though I knew that it was us making the current.

"Here, babe. Catch." Russ threw something white at me. It slapped my hand, but I dropped it even before I caught it. His underwear. The kind with red and blue stripes at the top, the kind that says he's a decent boy whose mother takes care of him.

"What happened, scared?" he said.

"I let them drown," I told him. "It was more merciful that way."

His skin looked green as old metal under the pond water. Like the dolphins in the fountain at the capitol. Or the Statue of Liberty. I couldn't help looking. But it was all mysterious. Waving in a dreamy underwater waver.

"Did Ada kick her out?" I said.

"No, she just told your dad to drive the chick home. Then old Ader put on her skinny pants and went out with Larkin to play pool."

"Oh." I dipped my head back into the water and flattened my hair into a smooth, satisfying tail, closed my eyes in the sun, then decided just to ask him. "Is that why you wrote the letter and all? Because of Daddy and Ada?"

He picked up a piece of pond moss and draped it over his

shoulder. "Letter?" he said. "I don't write letters. I'm the illiterate one, you know."

"Letter. The letter where you do, like back there."

"You won, all right, bitch? Just don't be telling the folks about it. Life's bad enough as it is."

My heart fell down a flight of stairs and flew up again. "You didn't write the letter?"

"What? What letter? Someone trying to blackmail your dear old dad?"

"Nothing like that," I said. "Are you sure?"

"I lie, all right? But not about politics. Just about sex. The old lady taught me that."

He flicked the moss at me and turned back to where his clothes were. Walking out of the water, St. Peter on the waves. His ass was so skinny it didn't even start till it was almost over. And his shoulders moved like switchblades–X-acto knives–delicate and dangerous and sure. I kept staring at him even after he turned around to put on his raggedy jeans. Then I saw all of him, and it wasn't what I thought, just a patch of brown curls over a few loose bags of leftover skin.

xi

You probably won't believe me, but I'd never seen a naked man before. Or maybe you will believe me, because that's what you were counting on. Sometimes my father would come out of the bathroom with no clothes on–that's true–but he'd cover up quickly and all I could remember was a confusion of shapes more complicated than skin was supposed to get. Like the bumps and bubbles on sugar toast or the texture of a stained glass window. Even worse, sometimes it made me think of a girl on our block who was born without an arm and how the skin waffled up in pink ridges around the stump of a bone when she took off her prosthesis for us to look.

Later, when I took biology and straightened out the symmetry in my mind, I figured it was like a roller skate, with the two industrial-strength wheels in front and the short rubber stop under the toe. Sharp, strong, efficient–something I could ride on for hours. And after I left the rink, even, when I felt the phantom wheels beneath me, and walked without slumping my shoulders or swaying my back, ladylike, for a change, as Ma'am would say.

Then came your letter, and the guns and knives and rapists. So I changed my mind one more time. Maybe it was violent, like they say. But no one told me, ever, that the penis has softer skin than a third-grader's earlobe, that it's so fine I can see blue veins through its damp pink tissue paper sheath, that it has a tiny, sticky mouth that opens as gently as a fish's gill, that when I put my cheek to it, I can feel the blood brimming in the veins.

Maybe that's because you're not supposed to tell me. Maybe that's what I'm not supposed to know.

But Russ didn't seem to mind much, one way or another.

He let me look for as long as I wanted.

"Only it costs a quarter," he said. "If you want to touch."

"No thanks," I told him. "I think I've had enough of that for one day." I stepped up to the bank and wrung out the skirt of my dress, a section at a time, squeezing so tight my fingers went numb. My father squeezed my fingers like that. Once when Dot had a solo in the school play and he was afraid she'd miss the high note. When my best friend gave me a bloody nose and I came home crying into a wet paper towel. When we watched election returns on TV. Or when he showed me how to use a gun. He didn't even know he was hurting me, like that. And I was too proud to say. It started with Daddy's hands—short, wide, with thick, stubby fingers. Something was wrong with the thumbs too. They bent forward instead of back, fat and stubborn as wine corks in cheap green bottles. My grandfather had the same thing. Ma'am checked our hands as soon as we were born, she said, to make sure we didn't have the Martin thumb.

Those thumbs made Daddy strong and clumsy, but they made me sorry for him too. And I wondered if he hurt my mother like that, or Joan or Ada. Because I knew he seemed graceful to other people, folding his hands together in a church-and-steeple knot, then opening them out again when he came up with a totally unexpected concept, uncorking his thumbs and letting the idea fly off like a dove. Making long, intricate speeches without notes. Traipsing one mistress right into another one's house, then forcing everyone else to deal with it. Like it was just our problem if we thought anything was strange. Clumsy and graceful. The way politicians were. I turned up the hem of my dress and looked at the handwork my mother had done on it—so much more precise than my father and so much less effective. I ripped straight up from the seam and the cloth tore with a breathless gasp, like a whip moving through the air. I did it twice more. By that time, Russ was dressed again, and sitting back against the tin tool-shed, and I motioned for him to scoot over so I could sit there too.

It was almost full noon. The sun throbbed against my face and the metal behind me; the whole world seemed to vibrate with heat, until I could see its lazy folds moving through the windless day, wrinkling the landscape. I felt chilly and warm inside my wet clothes. The skirt of the dress was already getting lighter, returning to its regular blue, but the padding of my bra clung in a soggy plaster cast over my chest. It'll be the last thing to dry, I thought, and I'll have two big wet spots under my clothes. There were still goose bumps on my arms, but I could already feel myself beginning to sweat behind the knees. Russ thumped his fingers on his chest, rubbed the tops of his thighs, reached down and hooked a hand around my ankle.

"Prickly pears," he said. "I like that."

"You would," I told him, but didn't move my leg. "Do you think my father is in love with Ada?"

"What's that supposed to mean?"

"Well, does he want to marry her?"

He jiggled my ankle. "Does she want to marry him?"

"She can't. He's already married."

"Well, there you go. I guess it doesn't matter, babe."

"I don't think people should get married. Not my parents, anyway."

"Too late," he said. "Besides, if they didn't do that they'd just do something worse. I bet we're really in hot shitwater now."

"Did he come back after he took Joan home?"

"Who?"

"My father."

"Look, Libby, he just keeps coming back. That's the problem. Don't you think we're in enough trouble now? You know they're going to blame it on me, don't you? Old

Tom'll be getting ready to put my nuts in a slingshot."

"So, do you think he's doing it with Joan too?"

"Not anymore. Or at least not much. The chick looks pretty desperate to me."

The pressure of his hand on my ankle was turning to a slow burn and I pushed it away. "How can he do that?" I said. "She's almost as young as me."

He picked at the shreds on the hem of my dress. "What's the worst part about making love to a five-year-old?" he said.

I stared at him, trying to make my blush stay down by concentrating on one ugly pimple.

"You're supposed to ask what," he told me.

"OK, what?"

"When you hear the pelvis crack."

Somewhere inside me, a gear slipped, organs that weren't even supposed to touch flopped together, and my stomach made a sizzling noise.

"That's it," I said. "I'm running away."

"I hate to tell you, babe, but you already did that. You stole a vehicle and abducted a minor. Now all that's left is to turn yourself in, like a good girl."

He was right. I was too straight to go any further. And I hated my parents for training me to be like that, weak and orderly and obedient as a dog. Ada's dog again, I thought, and wondered if Daddy ever felt that way too.

"Well," I said. "Let's do something else first. Let them worry a little."

"We could check out the ark over there. Did you ever get laid in a boat? Oh sorry, I forgot. Anyway, it's not so great when it's only a dry run."

I ignored him this time and we got up and walked through another patch of trees. The leaves were dingy–half gray, half green, and the air smelled sharp as gunpowder in the middle of May. On the ground I saw an open seed pod, some BBs, a used firecracker shredded up like a

126

frill on a party favor, thick bits of broken china.

Russ saw the china too, and stopped to put on his shoes, standing on one leg at a time while he pulled open the tongues and lashed up the laces. Shoes without socks. That always made me think of a guy you couldn't trust. That and dirty fingernails. A mustache darker than his real hair color. All of which was the opposite of my father with his clean habits and snappy little outfits. But I was getting to where I didn't trust him more than anyone else.

I squeezed my toes into my pumps and catapulted toward the next clearing. My leg was still sore, and the heels made walking even more difficult. But I didn't want to give Russ the satisfaction of thinking he'd hurt me.

"Ow," he said. "I think we're limping a little."

"It's these shoes. That's why you guys like them. It makes it easier for you to chase us."

I came up to the edge of the trees and stopped: out there, in the sparse prairie grass, was a houseboat on bricks. It looked as big as the statehouse in the middle of the field like that, although I guess it probably wasn't even as big as our house at home. Someone had painted it a sickly green– the color of wilted spinach left over in some side pocket of the refrigerator–and it was covered with pictures and letters and graffiti-type diagrams. But all of the colors were tainted, a tone too loud or shady, like vegetables just past their prime. And at the prow was the bust of a Viking goddess–pink coils of hair like rams' horns, orange lips, green, star-shaped nipples.

I wobbled on my shoe and caught onto a tree trunk for balance. The thing was so weird that it almost seemed familiar.

"They let him have that out here?" I said.

"Why not? It's better than a scarecrow, I guess. Besides, he's loaded. They'd let him have an alligator farm if he wanted."

"Who is he?"

"Name's Cyril Whitehead. Some cranky millionaire fundamentalist genius. First, he's an Indian and he got money from that. You know, this reimbursement they give you for being here first and getting fucked out of your property? Then he inherits all this wampum from some second cousin who made it big in petroleum by-products."

I scratched my hand on the tree bark, trying to get rid of the itchy feeling of asking something I didn't really want to know about. "But why's he live out here?" I said.

"You don't understand. He's always lived here. Besides, he's got relations and chickens and things. He's got a project now, and that might take him a while."

As we walked closer, I saw that most of the writing looked like math problems–numbers, symbols, sets and subsets, parallelograms. Even the pictures were a kind of math, with naked stick people intersecting each other at odd angles, some even disappearing into their own mouths. Or else in trick pony poses with a bear or buffalo or mastodon. They were all connected in lines and rows and circles. What they were connected by were the penises, which came out looking like crossbows. Or like plus signs, holding together the equations. That's why boys like math and we don't, I thought, and my mind peeled back a layer, to the quick. They think they're connecting the world together, the way my father connected all of us.

"Do you get it?" Russ said.

"What's to get?"

"Cyril says all this is supposed to bring rain. That or the apocalypse, I guess."

I ran my finger over the paint, which was thick and sticky as plaster tack. I could see bugs caught in the design, their legs fanned out in flattened distress signals. "Does he actually believe in that stuff?"

"Search me, Lib. Says it, that's all I know."

I kept looking at the pictures. But what really interested me was the writing which broke through the math graph every now and then like a morning glory through a chain-link fence: "And the Red Sea parted like the legs of the Scarlet Whore of Babylon and Moses knows where the pathway leadeth." Then there was a saying too high for me to read. So I took off my shoes and started up the ladder at the side of the boat.

"Now where are you going all of a sudden?"

"Up," I said, and before I was there, I could already feel his breath all gritty on the soles of my feet. But I still couldn't read anything, since the lines were in a strange language with triangles and saucers and waves where the letters were supposed to be.

"Hey, you can't read that. It's Hebrew."

"How do you know?" I said. "Maybe I took it in school."

"All right, so what does it say?"

"It says give me a little more space," I told him, but then I found something I could understand without faking it. "X-acto," it said in plain black letters to the side of the Hebrew. My toes clamped harder onto the rung of the ladder, and I felt the warm metal freeze on my skin. I looked again. It was still there, but it had moved under the Hebrew and down the side of the boat. Then up and to the center. My stomach swayed inside me like an empty swing that someone had just jumped out of. I thought I could make it stop if I could only get the letters to stay still.

Russ was still talking down below me, but it sounded odd, inhuman–crickets crawling in and out of their song. At first it was distracting, but then I thought stay with it, Libby, ride with it, then you'll be able to keep your balance. Graceful and clumsy, like the politicians. My arms shook and my leg vibrated where I'd strained the muscle, all along the line of my old scar. It felt beautiful and silver as a tuning fork. I'm a tuning fork, I thought, and the music is this silver pain.

I'd always wanted to faint, like the women in long, dizzy novels of love and betrayal, spinning in glassy spirals of desire. But now that it was really happening to me, I'd rather stay awake and see how it happened. I didn't go completely unconscious either, like I'd expected. There was just a gap of time where I wasn't there with Russ anymore. I was seeing my father instead. Or a dream I had of him.

It was Thanksgiving and Ada was making dinner for us. But it wasn't turkey this time. She served up some kind of fleshy fish that we had to peel off the spine like bits of prickly pear.

"Better than turkey," Daddy said. But as he swallowed the first bite, a tear opened in his throat and he started to bleed.

I didn't want to panic him, but I couldn't stop myself from screaming. Then Ada came running to the table and held a white cloth napkin up to my father's throat.

"Call the governor," she told me, and I went to the phone but I couldn't dial the number. I didn't know why I was calling the governor or what I was supposed to say if I ever got hold of him. And all the time there was a piece of flesh in my mouth, thick and rubbery as a chunk of dried-out cheese, and I was afraid to taste it.

When I came to, I was standing on the ground again, with Russ holding me up against the side of the boat. My mouth felt like I'd just broken an egg yolk in it, and Russ reached in and pulled down my bottom lip, dabbed at it with his shirttail.

"You bit your tongue," he said. "Lucky for you, I didn't let you swallow it."

"Gee thanks," I told him. "I guess you want a Purple Heart for that."

"No, maybe just a valentine, huh Lib? So what's wrong with you?"

"Nothing. I got dizzy. I fainted. Didn't you ever see anybody faint before?"

"Not like that," he said. "We don't faint out here in the wild west."

"Shh. Be quiet. I don't want someone to hear us."

"Why not? It's only Cyril and the pheasants."

Cyril. It even sounded like a serial killer. I shut my eyes and tried to recover from my faint. Cyril Whitehead. I didn't think my parents had ever talked about him. Or if they did, they never mentioned any ark. Why does he pick me, I kept wondering. And then I started thinking about Russ, whether he knew all along that this Cyril guy was after me and that's why he brought me here. The sun broke in bright spokes and needles on the underside of my eyelids and I tried to run.

But Russ saw what I was doing and blocked me. And everywhere else I looked this big ugly boat was in my way. I remembered a song from Sunday school: "So high you can't get over it. So low you can't get under it. So wide you can't get around it. You must come in at the door." I remembered playing tag in the churchyard, how my heart plunged down and up like a crooked pogo stick, and went so fast that my feet, burning and stinging in patent leather, couldn't keep up with it. How the weeping willow was home base, but I pretended it was heaven with its angel hair fronds reaching out for me. And whoever chased me was the devil, pumping hard, breathing steady. I ran until I felt fine glass splinters shooting into my lungs and I couldn't pretend anymore that it was only a game.

Then I found the end of the boat and turned around the corner. My heart stopped before my feet did. Because lying there on a narrow bed of bare springs was a dark man in cutoff overalls and no shirt.

And Joan was there with him, sitting at the foot of the bed with her arms gripping the bedframe behind her and her stocking feet plunged into his crotch.

xii

Before I could see anything else, a molting pink-and-white chicken flew up off the bedframe and headed for my face. It veered so close I smelled the quicklime, vegetable slop, and bird slime I remembered from my grandparents' chicken yard. Then I screamed and ducked, but it grazed my hair anyway, where I was afraid it would get caught the way a grasshopper did when I was seven years old, trapped in the tangles because I didn't comb my hair all the way through, like Ma'am was always telling me to. The grasshopper didn't move. I didn't move. We both sat waiting in rhythm. Then, as if on signal, it spit in my ear and I clawed at it until it was only sweet grass stains on my hand. Afterward, I wiped it off on a maple leaf and sat on my swing set and cried.

I wasn't afraid of animals, like people thought—it was just that I was always worried they were going to die around me, mash up against the windshield, squish under my feet, crawl out on the carpet to rot beneath the coffee table. It was a little like the way I felt about boys. They were too violent and vulnerable to be around, and it made the joints of my fingers and the underside of my tongue itch, trying to keep from cutting into them. But I knew I didn't want to do it, and I didn't want anyone else to do it either. Because I couldn't stand to be around and look at the mess.

The chicken landed safely on the ground beside me.

Russ touched my elbow so lightly I couldn't tell what he meant by it. Protecting me, hiding behind me, or holding me back.

Then I looked over at them anyway, Joan with her head

at the foot of the bed, and the dark man at the other end. She turned toward us, but didn't move her feet away from the stranger's crotch.

"Welcome to the summer home, kids," she said. Her ghostly blond eyebrows lifted and tweezed together, a fine gold chain that had gotten broken in the crush, and she gave an extra little jab with her toe, just showing off, I thought. "I think this is going to become campaign headquarters in the off-season. At least, our colleagues keep showing up around here."

"Libby," the man said. "Libya. Go ahead and come closer. Set your eyeballs on fire, honey. We're doing this for you." There was a wet shiver to his voice, as if he were sucking the juice out of the words as he spoke them.

I'd hardly looked at him yet, except around the edges, enough to tell I didn't want to see him all at once. So I started from one end and went back to the other, the way I used to eat a gingerbread man when I was small. First, Cyril's feet with their long, thin toes and cloudy nails like grains of corn turned to hominy, the second toenail in each foot bruised the green-black color of horseflies. Then the hair, black with a red gleam, one tiny braid of it twisted with twine and hanging crooked from a damp pink part. Back down to his legs, stringy and lean, with calf muscles suspended in their loose sacks of skin. And now up again for the first real feel of his face, where the slice of mouth and nose seemed out of sync with his round brown eyes radiating a green and shaky rhythm. His thighs were thin under the baggy cutoffs; the bare chest and arms strained with small, bitter muscles the size and shape of crab apples. Finally, right in the middle of him, where the gingerbread man snaps in half, he wore a paper napkin like a loincloth, fastened around his overalls with a serpentine silver chain.

"It started with Larkin," he said. "And it just got worse from there. Drunkenness. Deception. Corruption. Adultery. But I don't need to tell you, do I, angel? You've got an eyeful of sin. You took the beam in the eye, didn't you?"

"What?" I said.

"Your father. Mr. Beam-in-the-Eye. Mr. Him-Heap-Holi-er-than-Possum."

His legs wove open and closed over Joan's in the hypnotizing motion of a loom. I thought about the iguanas in Russ's bedroom and the writing on the rape note and the intersecting pictures on the ark. Evil was complicated, they always told me at church, and hell was some kind of machine like a factory furnace where everyone got intricate punishments to suit their particular sins. My mother knew exactly what would happen to us if we lied to her or hid our church money in the seat covers of the car or talked behind our girlfriends' backs. "Your circle in hell," she'd say, and tell a story of a spanking machine or money tree or whispering gallery. My guts expanded and twisted inside me when she talked about it. But heaven–heaven was just plain–good was only ordinary. When I thought of it, I felt a prickle in the back of my throat–the beginning of strep throat–and all I could picture were clouds and ice cream and puffs of cotton candy. The worst part is, you can't see through good, so you can never know if there's anything going on underneath it.

But with evil, there was a definite substance. Or at least a sound, like the seesaw grating of the bedsprings that was all I could hear for a stretched-out minute.

Over on her end, Joan's eyes were half-closed, but the dimples in her thin arms moved as she pressed against the iron bar at the bed's foot. Her dress jacket hung over the bar too, the blue silk showing up clay-red rust spots in the iron. I was surprised that she'd be that careless; then I thought about the shape my own dress was in, and a few rust stains seemed unimportant. Was Joan in trouble too, and was I supposed to save her? She looked calm enough, a princess taking a slightly distasteful beauty treatment. Something that could practically happen while she slept.

"What do you know about my father?" I said to Cyril.

"Daddy? The Right Honorable Jehoshaphat? Everything. Whatever you want."

I pressed my fingernails into my palms and concentrated on the half-moons I was making there, sharp and singular as cheese gratings. "What do you know about me?"

Cyril jostled Joan's legs a little more roughly; the springs sank lower and the song rose higher, in a jawing country twang.

"No one else thinks I need to know," I said. "No one else thinks I can handle any information at all. Anyway, how come you know all this stuff?"

Cyril turned to Russ, loosening his leghold around Joan. "Wheels in two-wheelers. Harpies in the sky. You're Ada's other son, aren't you? Spawn of the whore of Alcatraz? Nice to see you again."

"Hey boatman," Russ said from behind me. "I'd shake your hand, but I don't want to get any jism on me."

"No danger there." Joan ran her foot down Cyril's leg and pulled herself into a sitting position against the iron bar. "Cyril doesn't come. He's saving it all up for some definitive existential blowout."

"No kidding." Russ looked sideways at me, his face turning dirty pink, all except the skin around his pimples, which stayed white as dried glue. "So how's he do that?"

Cyril shifted on the bedsprings, brought his shoulders up higher against the headbar, poked his discolored toes through the honeycomb holes in the springs. Maybe that's how he got those bruises, I thought, pinching his toes like that. But then, the dark swellings that made his nails bubble out like the backs of water beetles seemed more serious, as if it would take something more frightening to make them rise.

"Tantra," he said, very fast, like a sneeze or an "amen."

Russ leaned closer to me. "Tantrums, huh? I'm good at those. Right, Lib?"

I wanted to push him away, but I thought I might need him on my side. "If that's what you want to call it," I said.

Joan twisted her hair up into the beginnings of a French braid, tucking in the stray hairs with her fingernails. "Pay attention, kids. This is a bit of information every red-blooded teenager ought to get a health pamphlet on."

"Tantra is spiritual sex," Cyril said, swaying on the bed-springs again, working up a rhythm. "Orgasm in the ozone layer. There's no wastage or abuse, the way you see in our current governmental practices."

Russ was breathing in my ear. "So what's government got to do with sex, Mister?"

"Don't start with me," Joan said.

And Cyril went on.

"It starts at the base of the spine, where the hipbone is connected to the body politic. You can ask Senator Martin about that. We had a demonstration in the governor's chambers and he wound up going home with the demon-stration model."

"So the guy fucks around," Russ said. "So what?"

I felt a lacy edge of acid in my stomach. I wondered what Cyril was doing in the governor's office. And I hoped it wasn't any worse than that. "What else?" I said.

"Sacred fluid, Libya. A man can make it rise up his spine, chakra by chakra, the way Moses charmed a snake up a pole for the children of Israel." He locked his hands behind his back and pointed a finger up along his vertebrae. Then he pushed it all the way up to the nape of the neck, so that his arms and shoulders twisted back like a ram's horns. His chest muscles strained out beneath the overall bib, and I saw his hard breasts, larger than I'd thought at first, with dark, miniature nipples and a long, flat gully of a cleavage.

Russ was getting impatient, fidgeting with my elbow. "But hey, why would you want to do that? It sounds pretty hoary to me. Like the dry heaves or something."

I wished he'd shut up. He reminded me of Dot, always

pretending to be mature, always asking adult questions I didn't want to hear the answers to yet.

Cyril had one hand around his neck now, and one still behind his back, so stiff it looked like it was tied there. "Given what you've seen of the world so far," he said, "do you really want to mix your seed up with it?"

No, I thought. I didn't want to mix anything of mine up with my father and the governor and Ada. Then I realized he meant Russ, not me. I didn't have any seed to spill, like they say in the Bible. I didn't have a choice.

"OK," I said. "I give up. What did my father do?"

Cyril gripped the sides of the bed and worked himself up off the springs, comb by comb, with the noise of a boy climbing a chain-link fence. Then he landed standing in front of me, shorter than Daddy, taller than Russ or Maury, his mossy teeth level with my nose. He smelled of sawdust and gasoline, and up that close, his skin looked young and rubbery, all except for the cobweb wrinkles threading out from the corners of his eyes. He nodded forward, swaying from one foot to the other, as close as he could get without actually touching me. "Libby," he said. "My Libyan Sibyl, with a hymen as sensitive as a hymn. Don't you know? You've been watching him all along, just like I'm watching you."

That's how he knew who I was. He'd already seen me–my ring, my breasts, my legs, my choir robe. According to your note, anyway. And it was true–I always thought someone was watching me. Even before the note. When I was nine, when I was twelve. Chewing on a rubber band or hanging upside down on the monkey bars although I didn't have any shorts on under my dress. Stroking the fine hairs in my armpit, trying to decide whether to let them grow. Counting the accordion pleats between my legs after I heard a lady in the church basement say she was glad she had all boy babies–girls were too messy with all those folds. Always, ever since I could remember, there was a look I felt on my skin like the sticky tape of a Band-Aid pulling away, dragging open the hair follicles, leaving me more naked than I was before. The look had a voice that came with it: "She touched her lips to the chalice," it said. "She rubbed the powder into her thighs." It sounded so deep and damp and tender that it fell apart while I was listening, disintegrated into shivers in my ears, dripped like expensive perfume down my neck, landed in a perfect bead of silence on my spine.

The voice was the same as his. But what Cyril was saying was obscene; not what my voice would tell me at all.

"Senator Martin. Turnover Tom. You don't really like the man, do you? How could you, a girl with pristine tastes like yours? He loves power, but he doesn't know what it is. He wants blood, but he doesn't like to have to smell it. He sets up the kill, then he's afraid to apply the blade at the right moment. Makes you squeamish, doesn't it? All those half-dead bodies lying around the house?"

"No one's dead," I told him. "No one's hurt. Nothing's happened yet." But I knew it was a lie. Things were happening before I got the note, before I could remember.

Cyril set his hand on my shoulder, so that I had to keep myself from jerking away. I pretended that if I didn't react, he wouldn't hurt me. His breath was thick on my face: a combination of red meat and sour cream with something medicinal mixed in between them. His hand pressed down on my shoulder blade, making me feel lopsided on my feet. But I still didn't move.

"Daddy backed out of the bargain. That doesn't surprise you, angel, does it?"

The chalk of my skeleton creaked inside me, as if all my bones were agreeing.

"Does it?"

"You don't surprise me either, Mr. X-acto," I said.

A lump moved along his jawline, and I had the feeling he was going to hit me. I wanted him to hit me, the way I wanted my mother to hit me when I got her so angry that she was afraid to. A nerve would chime between my shoulder blades, and I'd feel my body go numb. Then I knew she couldn't get to me, but only slap away at the surface. Because you don't hurt people by hitting them: you only hurt them by holding still.

Cyril finally moved; he gripped me around the waist and lifted me onto the raised bar at the head of the bedsprings. The rusted metal gristled against my thighs and the bar was so narrow I could hardly balance. I grabbed onto his shoulder. I wasn't sure if I was driving–steering–or only hanging on. I wanted to turn up his curled shoulders, unbend them, like the horns on my bicycle. When he pressed against me, I almost thought I could.

"You wouldn't turn tail on a bargain, would you, Libya?" he said, standing there beneath me. He pulled my knees apart, as simple as breaking open a dinner roll. Then he moved his hips in between them, and the chain of his loin-cloth slithered cold against my thigh. It felt raw and twanging. Frightening, but powerful too. As if no one had ever touched me before. As if no one else had ever told me the truth.

Cyril stroked the inside of my thighs, half scratching, half tickling. At first, I wanted to rub where he touched me, to erase it, but I was too scared. I clamped my hands harder into his shoulders. I concentrated on the crooked part in his hair, the single wavy wrinkle in his forehead, the ache in my hands. Then my nerves fell together in one long surge. He edged a finger inside my underwear. Joan coughed. Russ swore. The chickens gabbled.

My insides moved like a camera. Click. One, my mother, with wide-eyed agates for bruises. Two, a girl with her arms cut off, initials carved into her breasts: me. Three. Ada and my father; my father and Joan. Click. Cyril. Click. Cyril. Click. You. The shutter stuck, stalled. A fear without a rhythm seeped over my body, bleached everything as pale as a boiled chicken bone, bright as the sun's shadow stuck in an eclipse. I thought I'd never move again and all of us would stay where we were until the Judgment Day. But I'd rather die, I thought, instead of this holding open, this pleasure without an end. Then I shivered and jerked my head away and it was done.

I looked down again. Cyril held the bloody tampon I'd pushed out of me. A dead animal. A swollen mouse caught by its tail in a trap.

xiii

Cyril raised the tampon to eye level and smeared some of the clotted blood onto his arm. Then he lifted his elbow up and sniffed. "Quality virgin cesspool," he said. "Vintage whore of Babylon for our times."

The blood wasn't all the same color; it went from a dull clay stain at the string to a fat crimson bulb in the middle, then soaked and wrinkled and dark as a raisin at the other end. It smelled of raisins too—cooking raisins being stewed for my grandmother's sour cream pie. And just by smelling it, I could taste blood under my tongue, in raw cavities, in the broken, sweet spaces where I'd bit my lip or burned my mouth.

My legs quivered beneath me, weightless and feathery spider legs trailing off the bedframe. But I tried to slip down and stand up anyway. So at least my dress would fall back over my lap without me having to make a point about reaching down and covering myself up.

Cyril pushed his hand into the middle of my chest and propped me back up again. "Whoa, we're not finished here, Libya. We haven't even got to the sermon yet. First you've got your sermon, then you've got your mount."

"I just want a glass of water," I said.

"A glass of water? Sure you do. Just like our Lord. Only he went up to the well and guess what. Jack and Jill had peed in it. It was polluted by pullulation. Prostitutes and moneychangers and politicians. And their spawn. Only way to get that long cool dose of salvation was to drink it out of the stinking hands of a whore."

He grabbed my hand, uncurled it, stroked the fingers. "Sores of leprosy staring out from between the golden rings. Do you know what I mean?"

My mouth contracted; the sweet raw places stung. "I'm not a prostitute," I said.

He pushed his face forward into mine until our noses met, and the cartilage pressed down into the bone. I felt his face twitch and heard the teeth grating inside his mouth. I smelled kerosene and alcohol. I heard my sinuses click open inside my head. And I thought both our noses would have to break, splintered like crossed Popsicle sticks.

He finally moved back away. "No, you're not, are you? No, that's why you and me are going to hit the high walls of heaven together. You're a virgin, aren't you, honey?"

"Yeah, a fucking prude cocktease," Russ said.

I tried to hold my head steady. "So I'm a virgin. What about it?"

"Nothing," Joan said. "Nothing about it. It's just nothing. You can get it fixed."

Cyril went back to stroking my hand. "I thought so. You smell like one. You've got the heft of one. It's not all those lilies of the valley or roses of Sharon they blubber about. Vinegar and gristle is what it is, if you really study on the question. Vinegar and gristle."

Joan moved into my line of vision, sat down on a ladder leaning against the back of the ark, and slid into her shoes.

"You know what it is?" she said. "It's being afraid to go to the mall and try on jeans because you cream into all the inseams. It's thinking horses are pretty because of the manes. It's mistaking your girlfriend's diaphragm for a retainer. It's holding your hairbrush up to your panties and wondering how it all works. It's having to get drunk just so you can push a tampon in. It's falling in love with your boss or your soccer coach or your father and wanting them to do it to you so badly you dream about stuffing broken glass into your cunt."

"You dreamed that?" Russ said. "Or you just made it up to sound good?"

"I did it." Joan stood up. "Don't press me, joe."

144

My stomach shrank; my organs gathered up into a fist. Maybe it was my uterus. In the films at school they always compared the uterus to a fist. Why a fist? I wondered. Why so violent and boyish? It was a uterus, after all. Make a fist, class. Show them your uterus. I once dreamed that my mother had a tin uterus, like an iron lung. I made it gleam in a hundred places by denting into it with my fist. Now my stomach shrunk even smaller. I was afraid Joan was going to leave.

"Where's my father?" I said.

Joan blinked, and Cyril's face changed, all the lines jumping into a higher focus, as if pulled to attention by a string. The string from a tampon, maybe.

"He's gone to prepare a massacre for you in the face of his enemies. He's spilling his seed on a cracked and hardened footpath. He's choking on the honeyed tongue of a whore. He's cracking locust shells in the desert. Libya, I wouldn't be asking where your father is. I'd be asking who he is."

"Who are you?" I said.

"I'm the son of a carpenter and a ghost. I'm the richest man in this county and the smartest man in the state. I am that I am. Or at least I am who I say I am and I say I'm going to save you."

"What a coincidence," Joan said. "That's just what Libby's father said when he took my virginity off my hands for me."

"Doesn't look like it helped much," Russ said. "Unless you used to be weirder."

"Try it and see," Joan told him. "I think it might do something for you."

"What are you supposed to be saving me from?" I asked Cyril. "Rapists? Murderers? Lobbyists?"

He turned my wrist over and gripped it tight. Then he marked it with the blood from the tampon. One line thick and smudged as if it were squiggled out of a paint tube.

Then a lighter one crossing it.

X. X-acto.

"Lust," he said. "Corruption."

I felt the sticky blood drying onto my skin, and I imagined that it was poison, that if I let it stay there long enough to dry, I'd never get out of here alive. But after that I thought how ridiculous, the blood came out of me, how could I be poison to myself? Then I remembered, way back, before I really even had memories, but just some sort of molten stories that seeped around under the crust of my everyday life. Way back, my mother was angry with me because I wouldn't stop sucking my thumb.

"You're going to kindergarten next year," she said. "Your teacher will send you back to preschool if you act like a baby."

She bought some brown, sticky medicine that came in a bottle like nose drops.

"Libby," she said. "I'm going to put this on your thumb now, and if you suck it, your mouth will burn like when you eat the hot sauce on your Daddy's tacos."

I nodded.

"I want you to know that I'm not doing this to punish you. I just want to help you stop. Understand?"

I didn't say anything.

"I won't do it unless you tell me it's OK."

"OK," I told her, even though I didn't mean it. "Can we play coyotes now?"

"As soon as we finish this," she said, and painted the medicine on my thumb, where it stained just a bit darker than my skin, the color of Ma'am's makeup. It smelled the same as the municipal pool when we went to visit our cousins in the summer.

Then Ma'am went to work and left us with our father. I snuck into the kitchen to find where she'd left the brown dropper bottle, in the junk drawer with the can openers and the birthday candles and the coupons. I flicked at the plastic dropper, which dimpled in like the nipple of a baby bottle. She was the baby, not me. I could do something to show her.

Dot had followed me into the kitchen.

"Here," I told her. "This is magic juice. It'll make you all grown up."

"Juice," she said.

"That's right. Hold out your tongue."

And I spilled a drop of it onto her pale pink taste buds.

She started to cry right away, in the loud dry pinwheels of people so young or uninhibited that they can start to howl even before they have the chance to work up tears. I knew Daddy would be there in no time. So I had to get my own dose fast. I squeezed one, two, three drops onto my tongue, where they bleached and blistered like a sunburn in my mouth. It hurt so much I spilled the whole bottle onto the floor. Then I tried to wipe it up. By that time, Dot was crying in elaborate roller coasters and Ferris wheels. Now I wished my father would come. I wondered what was keeping him. I put my arm around my little sister and tried to wipe her eyes. But that only made her shriek louder and pull away from me, the cool, fat baby fists beating against my arms and chest. So I lifted my hands up to my own face and felt how I was crying too. Then I found out why Dot was so upset. The medicine that stung my mouth could sting my eyes too. It was worse than shampoo, worse than the stuff they put in swimming pools. It made me think of peeled grapes, of statues without eyeballs, of the pink, pulpy crater left under the big scab I pulled off my leg. That's what it would be like under my eyes, I thought. That's how I'll be without eyes.

Daddy finally came in and took us to the hospital. But they said all he could do was feed us soda crackers and let it wear itself off. So we ate soggy crackers and cried all afternoon, even though the neighbor lady, a nurse on the night shift, called to complain, then came over and put cold compresses on our eyes. And Ma'am came home and took us out for ice cream, yelling at Daddy all the way to the drugstore in the car.

After that, I knew how it was to poison myself. So you could never scare me as much as you thought. You have a poison pen, it's true. But I have a poison thumb. It makes us even, in a way.

"Adultery," Cyril said. "Drunkenness and bile and vermin. Plagues of frogs and lizards in the well."

The blood was dried on my hand now, stiff as nail polish on the opal underside of my wrist.

"What do I have to do?" I asked him.

He stopped short, as if he had a longer sermon planned. But even though he wasn't speaking anymore, his body kept on swaying, working itself into the next turn.

"Knock and the sepulchre will be opened unto you. Seek and you'll find the answer already there, sitting on your chest and recycling your breath. Libby, hold out your hand."

He pulled something out of the pocket of his overalls and pressed it into my palm, closing his hand over mine. The thing was metal, with some sharp edges and some smooth. He gripped both hands over my fist and choked whatever it was tighter and tighter in my grasp. I thought of my father showing me how to use the gun, standing behind me and arranging my fingers on the barrel, the trigger, the shaft. I felt the same musical cramping in my hand, the same anger and love and frustration. Then Cyril let go and I opened my fist with the magnetic ache of a flower that wanted to fold back together. The fingers were stiff and white. And in the middle of my palm sat something that looked like a missing piece from one of Daddy's debate trophies.

"What is it?" I said.

Joan looked over. "A new kind of IUD?" she said.

Russ crowded in closer. "Nut-and-bolt case of a screwdriver. Comes in handy in an emergency."

Cyril shook his head. "That, brothers and sisters, is the real head of state. The instrument of governance. The scepter of Caesar. It's the hood ornament off the governor's limousine."

"No kidding," Russ said. "What are you doing with it?"

"I'm realigning the lightning rod of power in this state. And I need Libby to help me."

"What am I supposed to do?"

He stroked my hair. "Influence with a certain intransigent senator," he said. "Blood ties." He held the tampon higher.

"What if I don't want to?"

He gripped the cap of my skull in his palm. "Up to you. Wheel within a wheel." And he swung the tampon so close I could smell it again.

"I want to talk to Joan," I said. "I want to talk to Joan in private for a minute."

He slipped his thumbs under the dentist's chain holding up his loincloth, then let his hand drop down and finger whatever was underneath the napkin—gently, slowly—as if he could read the bumps and veins. My throat crystallized with a sudden coating of acid. I was going to throw up now. Either that, or hold it in and petrify my whole body.

"I'll be inside," Cyril said. He turned around and climbed up the ladder with a lopsided ease. The ladder swayed inward and squeaked against the side of the ark. I waited until he was all the way in, then lifted myself off the bed and stood on clumsy feet that felt like someone else's.

Joan rolled her eyes at Russ. "You too," she said.

"You want me to park in there with that Bible-dealing dude?"

"What do you think?"

"All right, but you owe me. You owe me big-time."

When he was gone, Joan finally blushed; pink streaked into her face slowly as water colors into good, thick paper.

She opened her purse and handed me another tampon. "Reinforcements."

"Yeah, what, so he can pull it out of me again? Don't look, OK?"

She turned her back and I lifted my skirt. I remembered when I had my first period, and I wanted my best friend to come in the toilet stall with me and show me what to do. But you can't ask people to help you with something like that. Not even if you're out in the country without any rules. I set one leg on the bedsprings and pushed the stubborn nose of cotton up into the sticky canal between my legs. My hands came away streaked with more blood, and I tried to wipe them on the rusty headbar of the bed.

"Do you really hate my father?" I said.

She buttoned her suit jacket. "He's my boss. I have to work with him. I have to learn things from him if I'm going to grow up and get out of this."

"But do you still hate him anyway?"

Joan stared at me a minute, then licked her finger and started rubbing the blood off my wrist. "Don't you get it, Libby? I love him. I love him."

I sucked my breath in, then concentrated on the bitter tuck of Joan's smile, the silk of her sleeve, the sweet smell of butterscotch pudding.

"Look, I'm going to the hearing now," she said. "I don't think he'll hurt you. I don't know for sure, but I don't think so."

"Joan," I said.

She resettled her shoulder pads. "What?"

"Did he hurt you?"

"Which one?" she asked. "Not that it matters."

Then she waved her purse at me, slapped it flat against her chest, and walked off across the prairie grass, her legs steady and straight as a mowing machine. She was the cleanest person I'd ever met, clean way down beneath the skin. Her hairbrush never had any hair in it; the mirror in her compact didn't smudge. Her desk smelled of furniture polish and she kept Handi-Wipes and cotton balls in the upper left hand drawer. Her makeup didn't show, and I only knew she wore any from watching her put it on. But more than that, she had a clean way of thinking, where ideas and people didn't rub up against each other and leave their sticky resin all over the margins. I couldn't believe she'd gotten my blood on her, or that she'd said those things about my father, or that she'd ever associate with Cyril in the first place. But I couldn't believe it about my father either, or even about myself and the things I'd done since I started finding out.

I went back over to the bed, sat down, jiggled the springs, tried to decide whether it hurt or not. Maybe. I couldn't tell, so I lay all the way down and hooked my fingers through the holes. The wire cut into me, but only in certain places–shoulders, hips and thighs–where I weighed the most. It reminded me of the radiator grate in my grandparents' kitchen floor, where Dot and I used to lie in the morning before anyone was awake, playing that we were FBI spies being tortured on a bed of nails. The grate sectioned our backs off into strips of scorched bacon and warm milk, and whoever gave in first had to be a Russian for the rest of the day. In the guest room off the kitchen, our parents would be somewhere in between sleeping and arguing. We tried to ignore Ma'am's voice, hotter than the skin on our grandmother's hot chocolate, sharper than any of the radiator's spines. "The rigors of conjugal love," she told us once, coming out of the bedroom in a yellow nylon gown with bumblebees embroidered on the shoulder. "Someday I'm going to teach a course."

I locked my heels into the honeycomb of the springs and rocked even harder.

Then a loud noise cracked open the silence of the field. A crack, a cough, and an echo, like a car backfiring. Or a gun going off. All my limbs jerked up in different directions, and I tried to scream, but the only thing that came out was an empty hiccup. Now was the time to climb up the ladder, if I was ever going to do it. I ran to the ark and swung myself onto the first rung. I wasn't going to faint this time; I was too scared to faint. My blood was too thin and my brain too flat and unfevered. There was more space between the rungs than I thought, and it made me miss a beat every time. But I was pretty fast anyway, and scatted up without pausing until I was at the very last rung, where I turned, hanging half off the ladder, and looked out over the whole field, its grays and browns and golds running into each other, gradated, like the loops of color in a lake.

Out near the whitish pond where Russ and I had gone swimming, I saw a man and a woman: his navy blue jacket, her silver-blond hair. They were hugging, or fighting, or both; the motion of it was sharp and jagged as a pair of scissors. Russ's garden shears tearing up the leg of his jeans. I couldn't stop looking, even though I didn't want to know. I shouldn't look back, but I shouldn't go on either. So I hung there, tasting salt, smelling my own sweat like iodine and pineapple, frightened to move either way. Then there was another shot. I fumbled over the railing and ducked into the door of the ark.

xiv

I'd always believed people could disappear into vacant lots, fall into secret passageways that led them away from their families forever and into the fairy tales they didn't want anyone to know about. In our neighborhood, we had three of them, like completely different countries. One was a rain forest, with nude white tree trunks, water roots, glossy leaves that felt like photograph negatives, thick purple violets wet with dew against our ankles. Across the street it was the wild west: a patch of Indian maize, a beaten trail for our neighbor's minibike, a fort in the wide, low crotch of an elm tree. And if we went all the way to the bottom of our road, we could go to the races in any car we liked, a gentle white Cadillac with spots of rusted skin disease or a burgundy Mercury with a skylight ripped out of the roof in jagged lines, as if a giant did it with a can opener.

Once, our babysitter took us to that far vacant lot and it really happened: we walked past the junk heap, the five rotting cars, the tire swing, the pile of used bricks the color of earthworms and bubblegum and the bruised underside of a swollen lip. Then we were somewhere else, in a neighborhood we'd never seen before. The trees were a darker green, and the houses jutted too close together, like dogs nosing each other in the park. The sidewalk sank and cracked and billowed, as if there were something bubbling underneath it. A funny kind of plant, a long brown seed pod curved like an Arabian sword, was scattered all over the ground. Dot picked one up, peeled it open, and pulled shiny black nuts out of a sticky, green-smelling resin. She handed each one to me as she pried it out of the goo, and when we finally looked up we saw our pretty redheaded babysitter talking to a grown-up in sunglasses and a sheepskin jacket. His hair was the wet black of pencil lead, the kind that our school librarian said could poison you if you poked it into your arm. He had a beard with two licks of white in it, right where his mouth opened, like two mechanical springs. When our babysitter turned away from him, her hands pushing into her jeans pockets, the fringe on her Mexican poncho floating around her in a halo, he grabbed the tail of the poncho and pulled her back, reached around and gripped his hands over her breasts. We could see the two fists knotted under the rough, woven fabric of her poncho, and hear the gristle of his whisper grinding into her ear. Then he let her go, turned to me, and asked how old I was.

"Nine," I told him, even though I was actually ten.

"Sweet corn," he said, and squatted down beside me. He smelled the way the bathroom did after my father took a shower. He put his hand between my legs and pinched me through the ribbed skin of my corduroys, then held his fist up and showed me the tip of his thumb wedged between two knuckles. "I gotcha. What's that there?"

"What?"

"Your nose," he said, and laughed, sputtering up squiggly noises from his throat. "Come back when you're thirteen."

Then the babysitter steered one arm around me, one around Dot, and we walked away fast. She started singing a song about a papaw patch that had the same words over and over. Dot asked who the man was, but no one paid any attention to her, so she just gave up and sang along.

Afterward, I tried to go back, to find the sheepskin man, and figure out what he was talking about. But I couldn't remember how we got there. I'd go down to the vacant lot and twirl around until I was dizzy looking for the path we took. But I never found that neighborhood again. And by the time I was thirteen, I wasn't sure if we ever went there.

But I was convinced that any minute, accidentally, I could step through a bush or into a gopher hole and be as totally lost as I was before.

And that's what happened when I finally fell into the ark. I thought here it was, a place I might never have to get out of, where I'd never have to find out about what really went on with Ma'am or Daddy or Ada, or who shot the gun and why. I'd just go on with your story, as if I never had one of my own. That satisfied me—it made my fear all solid, instead of something that moved back and forth, warming and chilling me, sunshine through rain.

It was damp in there, and dark. The air fluttered between midnight and dusk, and bits of sawdust stung in my nostrils. It smelled of paint, wood shavings, and turpentine. But there were the regular human smells too—meat, sweat, pickles, beer. I turned around, adjusting to the faint static of light, until I found a crooked staircase lit with green and red light bulbs, fluorescent polyps growing at odd angles and showing up the graffiti on the walls. I went down three steps to read the stuff, then just kept on going.

Pulchritude is the rich man's poultry.

Jesus came to suck away the juice of the world.

If her tit offend thee, pluck it out.

Which made me think of you and your letter. Whether you'd walked down those stairs in front of me, or if you'd come on in after, or just walk along beside. Because that's where I felt you most, on the stairs between things, where your shadow cut into mine, and I turned numb wherever our edges overlapped. A crackling noise shook itself out of the dark, static flapping from the sheets on a clothesline. I stopped, listening for the direction it was coming from. But I couldn't tell, and nothing seemed safer than anything else. The way Dot almost drowned one summer out at Lake Arapaho because she lost her bearings and couldn't tell which direction to swim in to break the surface.

At least it wasn't a gunshot, I thought, and forced myself

to keep walking, gripping the hood ornament in my pocket, and feeling its complicated design folding in on itself. Too messy, with all those folds. And secretive too. I scraped my little finger against the rough edge where the ornament had been broken away from the governor's limousine. I tried to feel something. But I was too scared to wake up.

At the bottom of the stairs, it was like moving day in a junk store, a maze of furniture and boxes with no pathway cutting through. A grandfather clock that someone had repainted bright green and orange, without bothering to stay even with the lines of the molding. A headless dressmaker's dummy covered in feathers, a whole breastplate of duck and pheasant so perfect that I had to touch it, fanning out the fronds of a metallic blue tail feather, slick and fine and resistant, connected to its stem with dry white cartilage like the veins in a leaf. Then I flicked at a red weather vane with cardboard people at north, south, east, and west. As it turned, I saw that the two men and the two women were half-naked, each carrying something–a spear or animal or briefcase. I looked at the girl holding a cow's head by the horns and wondered if it was me. But I didn't want to think about it too much, so I turned to a refinished pulpit standing next to it. On the top of the stand was a dish drainer pasted over with a crust of sequins, three Bibles held open in its racks, all of them turned to the same chapter of Deuteronomy. And each chapter was marked with a hat pin at verse sixteen. A pocket knife sat on the ledge of the drainer. I picked it up, saw the Kiwanis symbol on the side, then put the knife in my pocket for safekeeping.

I moved over to a stash of cardboard boxes stamped "Galvin Petroleum Byproducts" on the side, and picked an old book out of one. *Masonic Codes*, it was called. The paper was yellow and smelled of strangers' basements; it left a chalky coating on my fingers when I opened to the spiked print and the line drawings of cathedrals and men in tights. Also in the box were *Prophecies of Nostradamus*, a couple of old hymnals, *The Horned God*, and a newspaper from the year before. It was folded to the "Local Scene" section and my father's face was there, circled with a red halo of highlighter. "Governor Welcomes Magnate's Offer." I looked more closely at the picture. Cyril was shaking hands with the governor, and Daddy was standing behind them, leaning on the fancy radiator that I recognized from the governor's office. The article said that Cyril Whitehead wanted to donate money to the state to finance an arts and agriculture program. Dams and irrigation systems that were actually works of art. Some experts suggested that this was highly impractical. Other people in the capitol just said there were bureaucratic problems with mixing two types of government activities. But the state needed the money, and the governor said they'd try to work something out. That was what Daddy always said too, when Ma'am and I had a fight: "Don't worry. We'll work something out." But it usually meant we were supposed to forget about the whole thing.

I set the paper on top of the pile of books on the floor. It made Cyril seem harmless. After all, he was dressed like a regular person in the picture, and he could obviously act rational enough to get into the governor's inner office. Maybe it wasn't so dangerous to be here after all. I went on digging in the box, pulling out more books about the Bible, witchcraft, ancient Greece, the Crusades.

Finally, the books gave out, and there was just the packing—individual plastic pillows sealed on all sides. I poked my fingernail into one and slit it open. Inside, there was a clear plastic balloon the size of a quarter. It had a thick rim rolled up around its sides. I slipped my finger into the opening, and the plastic felt as smooth and filmy as the skin of hot pudding, or the half-dollar hollow in my inner thigh. I popped the skin of one, then opened another. And another, like they were fortune cookies and I was hoping to find a message somewhere inside. I forgot about Cyril and my father and Joan, as if I were eliminating my problems one by one. I didn't care how loud I was, or who came to find me there. I only wanted to empty out the whole box.

When all the plastic was lying next to me in a litter of shells and broken skins, I still wasn't satisfied. I ripped down the sides of the box, as if I were peeling it open. The cardboard gave a corrugated growl. Someone was sure to hear me now.

But no sign yet. There was another crackle, sizzle, snap. They were in another room, where they couldn't hear me rustling around. Or at least, they could pretend not to.

I picked up one of the balloons and unfolded it completely. It stretched out longer than I'd thought. More like a tube than a globe. I thought of the shape of Russ's body. The contraption Joan was trying to tell me about earlier in the office. Plastic, petroleum, rubber, rubbers. I was sitting next to a pile of ruined rubbers. There was an ache behind my cheekbones, as if I wanted to blush. But how could I be embarrassed, I thought, after what had happened to me.

Instead, I piled all the books back into the box and dropped the trash in on top of it, handfuls at a time. Then I tried to shape it in a kind of pyramid. It worked well enough, but I needed something for the top. A single perfect condom. But I'd ripped all of them. So I pulled the hood ornament out of my pocket and stuffed it inside one of the broken ones. Then I set it at the peak of the pyramid, where it looked like some spooky, abstract Christmas angel. I stood back. The membrane glistened over the metal, and it did look like an angel, an angel caught in a caul.

I remembered the doll in the parking garage and hoped you were satisfied. At least, I was satisfied. Now you could wonder what I was thinking about.

Or maybe I'd trash the whole thing and the ark with it. I found my father's lighter and flicked it on, then held it over the pile of books. Burn up the whole thing and get rid of it. But then I'd never know. I pushed the flame under my best fingernail and thought about how long I could take it. The pain, I mean, but even worse, the suspense of waiting to grow up and lose my virginity and find out how bad things really were. The fingernail wouldn't really take flame, but only singed and darkened at the edges. Disappointing, like everything else. I moved the lighter closer to the bulb of my fingertip.

Then there was Cyril's voice again behind me. Starting at the base of my spine and shooting up into my nape, so that I pulled my shoulders back to catch it. "Libya. Sibyl. Don't fall into the snares laid by the harlots before you. The Lord has need of you."

At first, I thought I was only hearing voices, like those Catholic saints and the prophets in the Bible. But then I turned around and saw that he was actually there, standing over by a chandelier strung with gum wrappers and cigarette packages. His face looked chipped in the shadows, the forehead molded with many fingers, and fingerprints left sunk in the clay. His black hair floated away from his face like somebody drowned.

"More than that, I have need of you. What do you think you're doing here?" he said.

"Looking at your stuff. You've been spying on me for long enough."

He moved a step closer. "Did you find anything you liked?"

"Maybe." I put the lighter back in my pocket and sucked at my burnt fingernail. "You've got some pretty weird junk around here."

"The leavings of a denatured culture," he said. "Seedlings. Evidence. You weren't going to burn the evidence, were you?"

I shrugged. "Someone shot a gun out there, I think."

"People shoot guns in the country. They rape and pillage

and sodomize in the city. No surprise there. What's surprising is you. Now that I think about it, maybe you weren't going to burn my property. Maybe you were going to burn your hand? Is that it? Sizzling and frying of unholy loves? If your hand offend you, cut it off?"

My stomach pulled tight, but I couldn't let on. I remembered the hands in the note. "That's you, not me," I said.

"Let's see about that," Cyril said, and grabbed at the ragged skirt of my dress. I thought he was going to pull it off, but he only fumbled in the pocket and came out with the lighter.

"Give me your hand."

"Why?"

"You know, there's a hollow place in the flame. That's what your Shadrach and your Meshach and Abednego knew that Nebuchadnezzar didn't."

"He didn't know much anyway," I said. "Isn't he the guy that went crazy and ate all that grass?" I couldn't tell if my Bible knowledge was going to make things worse or better for me, but I couldn't seem to help showing it off anyway.

"That was just the pressure of power talking," Cyril said, and sat down on a wooden crate. "It could happen to anyone we know. Or worse. Come here, Libby. Sit on my lap. Let me show you the hollow place in the flame."

I balanced on the balls of my feet, ready to run.

"Come on, Libya, where are you going to go anyway? Mama's home in Purgatory. Daddy's out fishing for votes. And where's the little girl who looks after the sheep? She's under the senator fast asleep."

"What are you saying?" I asked, standing in front of him so that I felt myself swaying the way he did.

"I'm just telling you a story," he said. "The story of your life." Then he pulled me onto his lap. Not rough. Convincing. As if I had been missing all that time. His thick, smoky hair touching my cheek. His hipbone sharp beneath me. His bare legs sticking to mine.

"Here." He handed me the lighter. "Give me a light."

So I did, and he passed one finger through the flame, then two, then three. The fire glowed through the skin, and I could see the shape of the bones, their long shadows pulled across his face like claw marks.

"Air pocket. Oxygen hollow. Now you try. I know you're dying to try it."

I gave the lighter back and he shot the flame up too close to me, so that I felt the heat flap up against my cheek. I held my finger out and he dragged it through the fire, pinching the nerves open and melting the flesh into marrow.

"Ow, that hurt."

"It's supposed to hurt the first time. You have to try it again. Pain's a precise art. Pleasure's sloppy in comparison."

He took my finger through the other way, and this time it was as if the skin had sealed shut. But there was a throbbing from the inside, and I smelled something like raw liver being fried up with flour.

"Stop."

"You want me to stop? That's what your Daddy said when we found the trash on the governor. He backed out. He wouldn't play his hand through one more time. But I think you're different. I don't think you're as sloppy. Do it once more, Libya. Go on. Do it alone."

He touched my elbow and I lifted my hand. My wrist trembled. Under a few dried flecks of blood, the pulse sank and expanded like the throat of a bullfrog. Then I held my breath and flicked the same finger through the flame. Nothing. Just the same old burn glowing inside the skin.

"I did it," I said, and my brain rose, warm dough against my forehead. I realized I'd had a headache for a long time, and now it was gone.

"You found the hollow," he said. "I knew you weren't meant for the easy paths of whoredom." He tucked his hand into the top of my dress so gently he barely rippled the fabric. His fingers felt for my breast and gripped around the nipple, stroking it until I felt it change shape in his hand, poking against his solid palm. "You're like me, Libya. So don't try to deny me again." He pinched the nipple hard, then harder.

The pain was just an edge of ice, a pencil nub of pressure; then it scrawled through my body, blacking in all the lines.

"Stop it," I whispered through my teeth.

"You and me, clamped onto the tit of terror," he said, then reached around and rubbed my back with the other hand.

"Let go," I said, breaking away from him and standing up.

Cyril grabbed me again, came in so close I saw the stray gray hairs in his eyebrows, the pink, pulpy tear ducts in the corners of his eyes like the sting in a jellyfish. I thought he was going to kiss me, but then he ducked down and bit into my nipple.

I screamed. Or I tried to scream, but my voice only gnawed at the back of my throat. Sensation seeped away from me like radio waves, in circles, then came back in tight rings around both breasts.

"Don't worry, Libya. You'll learn to like that too."

"What are you doing? What do you want from me?"

"Why don't we just go in here and talk about it."

He walked me to the far end of the room and opened a door that he had to duck to get through.

"This way," he said, and I couldn't think of anything to do but follow him.

The next room curved with the hull of the boat, and Russ was there at its widest point, sitting on a camp stool in front of a tall lantern with a blue fluorescent tube. He was throwing something into it that made the crackles and sizzles I'd heard before. Electrocuting noises from one of those bug lanterns for outdoor parties. Next to him was a big white bathtub with black and purple stains running down its sides, lion paws settled on the floor. And next to that, a pulpit painted up like a totem pole, one red and black face over the other, with the last one hanging upside down.

Russ looked up, threw something invisible in our direction. "High times out there, huh? She going to put out for you?" He pulled at the ragged leg of his jeans, ripped off another tassel, sat on his hands. His shadow hung behind him on the wall, humped over and haggard as a library eagle. But underneath, he seemed small, sleepy, hungry, younger than me. My nipple throbbed, and I felt sorry for him, because he could never understand what happened with me and Cyril. Not if he wrestled with me till we were as old as Daddy and Ada. Not even if I let him win.

Cyril led me over to the lantern and motioned for me to sit on a stool made out of a tree trunk. The top was polished to show off its thick rings, and the base was carved with a design I couldn't make out. I sat down and tried to read it with my fingers, scraping them against the bark, as if it could tell me what Cyril would do next.

"Libby, I just want you to know that it was our legal oracle who suggested this tack."

"Who?"

"Lady Jane. Jeanne D'Arc of the Ark."

Joan. Whose first lover was my father. Who bought me my first bra. Who said I don't think he'll hurt you.

He pointed to the tampon lying on top of the lantern, drying out to brown now, with only a few loose strings of red left clinging to its sides. "So, do you have any idea what the blood of a virgin can accomplish?"

I reached down and scraped harder against the carved bark, trying to claw inside the trunk, which was only a trap door, I knew, into some uglier dream or story, where a man and a woman pulled their fingers through my tangled hair, put my eyes out, and led me to you.

XV

Walk a bleeding virgin over the fields and she'll make the crops grow. Mix her flow with her saliva and apply to mortal wounds. Stir her menstrual fluid into a man's beef stew and he'll love her forever, long after he's forgotten the strange metallic savor of the dinner. Paint her onto your fingernails and you can work miracles. Eat her out at the end of her cycle and you can join priesthoods and motorcycle gangs. Drink her out of a human skull at midnight and you'll never die.

But don't leave her to herself, or it could kill her.

That's what Cyril told me about my blood.

It could kill me, he said, by traveling up through my body like a wandering Jew, entering the sacred portals of breath, polluting the marrow, engulfing the chakra, seeping up into my head and giving me brain fevers.

He paced between me and Russ the whole time he was talking, and I imagined him as the hemoglobin, the hemogoblin doing all this devastation. Shuffling and swaying through my bloodstream, thumping on the bones, swinging on the circuits in my brain, cutting off the circulation.

I leaned forward and my nipple pressed into the side of my arm, swollen as a bee sting. Blooming like a blood blister. I remembered the country ticks in the woods by my grandmother's house, how they'd show up as scabs on our scalps, but on the cows and horses, who couldn't peel them off, they'd grow into clay-colored marbles hidden under an ear flap or hanging off a flank.

When she fed the cattle, my grandmother picked the ticks off as nonchalantly as picking grapes for jelly. She pressed her fingernail in to show Dot and me the thick red flow, the way we used to check the filling in a piece of chocolate candy, then wiped her hand on a feedsack. "Your grandfather burns them off," she told us. "But I just can't bring myself to do that to God's poor creatures."

That summer, I sat at my grandmother's gold-flecked formica kitchen table and drew while she made pies, gravy, butter, fried chicken. On the back of a Sunday-school lesson, I drew a cow with Popsicle udders. On the back of a train schedule, I drew a rabbit and a possum eating up the garden. And then, on the back of an advertisement for a dog show, I drew what was really bothering me–a huge round red blob, big as a garage door, attached to a tiny thumb-sized girl in doll clothes. The blob was the tick and the girl was me; you could tell by the red-and-blue culotte skirt and the lumpy braids the color of summer squash. When I showed the picture to my grandmother, she traced over it with her stiff, flour-covered fingers and pushed her reading glasses higher onto her nose. "Libby," she said. "Don't you think that old tick would just fall off and die if it got that big and heavy?"

But there'd still be so much of me in it, I thought. How would I ever grow back again? I pushed harder into my arm and wondered if it was really like Cyril said, that all that blood was collecting in me, taking me over, sucking me out like a tick from the inside. Sometimes, before my period, I felt that way, heavy and feverish, as if I were going insane, not because my mind was confused, but because my body was so full I didn't have room to think. My nose would get stuffed up; my brain would press against my forehead; my guts shifted around, making noises like a house settling down at night. And I'd sweat as much as a fat person, a thick syrupy smell, like Sunday ham cooked with pineapple and left out on the stove all afternoon. I was suffocating inside my own body, was what I thought. I'd lie on the floor of my room, press my stomach into a hard sofa pillow, and read a novel until I couldn't stand it. Then I'd try anything: Lying upside down, with my feet on the bed and my head on the floor. Plugging in my hot curlers, then rolling them, one at a time, over the tight places in my stomach. Finding splinters on the bottom of my dresser and poking them into my arm, just to keep my mind off things, to keep my mind on the surface, out here with me, instead of in there getting crushed by all the blood and bones and organs.

It didn't hurt, if that's what you're thinking. I'm not saying there was pain. But I almost wanted it to hurt, so there'd be a focus, so there'd be a way out, a puncture wound in the fuzzy, stuffed undergrowth of my body.

That's where you came in, I guess. I think I accidentally asked for you.

Russ signaled me from beneath Cyril's elbow. He touched his finger to his head, shrugged his shoulders, rolled his eyes. Maybe he was trying to tell me a way out.

But I wasn't listening to him anymore. I tucked my hair behind my ear and looked away.

"They cut one woman into twelve pieces and sent the remains to the leaders of the twelve tribes of Israel," Cyril said. "And that was enough to solidify political union in the Holy Land. Hell, she wasn't even a virgin."

She was someone's wife, I thought, and that was worse.

"Females don't have much use for blood, but it's a priceless resource for the rest of us."

Priceless. I was a pearl of great price, getting fat inside a sow's ear, like one of those ticks on my grandmother's cows. My skin felt phosphorescent, the membrane was stretched so tight over the burden of my worth.

"'Woman, you will suffer greatly in childbearing,' the Lord said. And that's what women do ever since. In and out of childbirth. In and out. They do it much better than men. Your father the senator, for example. You could outlast him in a fiery furnace any day."

But Cyril was the pearl of great price to me. The earring in the other ear, the only person I'd ever met who was horrible enough to meet my imagination. He was my match. He was my way out. He was going to save me, like he said.

"So," I asked. "What do I have to do to prove it?"

He stopped, his hands low on his hips. "First, let's get Dad involved in this." He leaned down and picked the tampon up off the bug lantern. "Any message you want to send the old sinner? Your father who art in session?"

"Yeah," I said. "Tell him I'm having a great vacation and I promise not to tell my mother."

Cyril smiled. "Did you hear that, you little blue-ball gargoyle?"

Russ flexed his fingers back, but the knuckles didn't crack. "Who? What? Are you talking to me?"

"Yes. You. Ishmael. Son of Jezebel."

"All right with the names," he said. "I hate to tell you what they call you up at the capitol."

"A prophet is without honor," Cyril said. "I hope you heard the girl because you're taking the message to Senator Martin and I think he's going to be interested in squeezing all the information he can get out of you."

"Yeah, I look forward to that."

"Unless you'd rather stay and become an accessory to the crime." Cyril unhooked the napkin from the dentist's chain around his waist and wrapped the tampon in it, as carefully as if it were a piece of cake or a ladyfinger at one of Daddy's political receptions. "This ought to get you through the secretary for a personal interview."

"Shit," Russ said. "Come on, you don't seriously want me to take that to him, do you?"

Cyril sat down next to Russ, gripped his wrist, and made him turn his hand over. "You don't seem like a mealy-mouthed, lukewarm guy to me. What happens to that kind, Libya?"

"The Lord spits them out," I said.

"Should we spit out your pal Beelzebub here?"

I looked at Russ and he shrugged again. "He's just a kid. I think he wants to go home."

"So the sibyl's spoken." He stuffed the napkin into Russ's hand. "Now, for authentication. Libby, will you go get the governor's hood ornament for me? The one you decorated up so pretty?"

I stood up and walked out into the room I thought I might never see again. Cyril's junk seemed comforting now, as if it would keep me company through whatever was going to happen. Then I saw the hood ornament gleaming on top of the pile of rubbers where I'd left it and went over to pick it up. It looked like an ordinary piece of junk to me, and I wondered what made Cyril think Daddy would recognize it. Unless they were together when Cyril stole it. Why would anyone steal a hood ornament in the first place?

I could probably get more clues while I was here. I started to open another cardboard box, then stopped and realized I could even leave if I wanted to. There were no locks, chains, ropes, gags. And the only guns I knew about were outside the ark, with Daddy and Ada and their friends. I tried walking toward the stairs, but the memory of Cyril held my nerves in a steady, glassy panic, like a cracked crystal goblet that still won't spill a drop of wine. Maybe it was my blood, like he said. Or maybe I just wanted to see how my father would react. I closed the box. I put the hood ornament in my pocket, then went back into the other room.

When I got there, Cyril was still giving Russ instructions. "And don't let him bring that Maury character, or the bitch goddess senator either. Just Lady Jane."

"Here it is," I said, and I felt an excitement that seeped outside my skin, and glowed in a halo all around me. Something was finally going to happen that would change me for good. "I want to write the note."

"Now you want to write a rape letter?" Russ said. "This is getting too gory for me."

"No, a ransom note. You know."

"Do we have to go get a bunch of newspapers and cut out letters and shit?"

I nudged into his side. "He knows who I am, Russ. That's the point. So he can recognize my handwriting and believe it's really me."

Cyril took the hood ornament and stuffed the tampon between two of its prongs. "Not a bad idea, Libya." He reached for a red felt-tipped marker that was clipped onto his overall bib.

"But write it," he said, "on something significant. Like the skirt of your dress."

I took the knife out of my pocket and pulled the skirt out tight. Then I slashed into it and ripped it the rest of the way, like my mother tearing my favorite sweatshirt into dusting rags when she was mad at me for skipping the worst parts of the housework. It had the sound of tire skids in it, and fan blades gearing up, and the bathmat being beaten on the wobbly front porch railing. It was the most violent noise I could think of—not a gun, not a chain saw, not a fire siren or a firecracker. Just someone's mother tearing cloth when she was mad.

I turned the fabric over, inside out, and smoothed it out on the stool where I'd been sitting. Cyril handed me a marker and I tried to think of what to say. There wasn't much room, and I realized I'd been saving up for a long time, waiting to write a leaving home letter, wanting to compose a suicide note, all the words laid out smooth and beautiful, like my body on the bed. The heading blank and mysterious as my face. Commas tossed around in careful disarray, like the ratty curls it took me so long to set in the morning. The signature posed just so at the bottom, one graceful foot sticking out of a long formal nightgown.

But when it came time, my letter wasn't that way at all;

it was rushed and short and ugly, something Cyril would write on the side of his boat.

"Turn the ship home," it said. "I know all about it and it makes me sick. Don't bother to save me."

It wasn't exactly a letter, but it still needed a signature of some kind. Not my plain family name, though, or–more formal–"Elizabeth." I wanted to show that something had happened. I wanted him to know I'd met Cyril.

So I made the sign of the bloody X Cyril had marked on my wrist. Still, I wasn't satisfied. "X-acto" would just be copying. I needed a different word.

"Ecstatic," I thought. "Extravagant, extortion, exterminate."

Then I wrote: "X-libris." Your daughter. Her book.

"That's it," I said. "See how he likes that."

Cyril put a hand on my head and stroked the hair, pressing my ear down flat. "Now go inform the officials, boy. They must be getting restless."

"OK, but I still don't think this is a great idea."

"You want to scare Ada, don't you?" I said. "You want to get rid of my father."

"I was thinking more like a hunting accident or a smear campaign."

"This is better. It makes for more interesting pictures on the evening news."

"I guess." He touched the ripped side of my dress, where my leg was bare all the way to the top of my thigh. "Are you going to be all right, babe?"

I felt tears needling the corners of my eyes. I was embarrassed to have him call me that, in front of Cyril. It was as bad as having a father. "Are you supposed to be my white knight now or something? That's a real change."

Russ blushed so that his whole face turned pink as his pimples. "Forget it. Sorry I asked. Have a nice crucifixion."

"Thanks for nothing, " I said.

"Same to you."

Cyril walked in between us and put one hand on my shoulder, one on Russ's. "Go in peace," he said. "And then return the pieces."

Russ rolled his eyes. "Whatever."

Then he walked out of the room and I watched his shoulder blades denting into his thin T-shirt, first one, then the other, at bent angles like the wings of a seabird you'd never expect to fly. As he moved, he seemed to clear up what I was doing, what I was supposed to do.

I remembered waiting in the airport once, when my father was coming back from Washington. A boy was cleaning the big picture window in front of the boarding strip. He held the window scraper at one angle, then another, timing the drips, drawing off the water. His shoulders moved into the glass and away from it, as if he were dancing with his reflection.

My mother was waiting in the car. Daddy's plane was late. I sat with my legs crossed so that I felt the itchy stubble where my calves touched. I'd only shaved my legs two, maybe three times, and I had to sneak Ma'am's razor to do it. So I waited a while between shaving sessions, to keep her from getting suspicious. But now the hair was getting long again and I felt like two people: the one the hair grew out of and the one it scratched against. I felt like two people and I didn't like either one of them.

The boy looked as if he knew how to use a razor, anyway. He drew the lather off the window with a flourish. He made it seem like a sport, not a job. That was the way with guys. They only played at things, pretending that nothing was serious, so if the razor slipped, it didn't count anyway. My father played and my mother drudged and they both got paid for it. But it made Ma'am mad—and that's why she was in the car now—because someone had called her at work about my father again. She never told me what they said, but I knew the kind of thing it must be. And I knew that afterward, she'd make us do even more housework than usual.

The plane droned into hearing distance, a loud lawn-mower on a hot day. It headed straight into the picture window and the window washer. The propellers on the plane, the shoulders of the boy, the blade of the window scraper. I wanted the plane to crash through the window. But instead, everything stopped and Daddy got out, the first person off the plane. He had on a striped suit, cracked black shoes, a red tie. And right behind him was Joan in a salmon-colored shirtdress, carrying a folded newspaper under her arm. She caught up to him and he said some-thing, then she tapped him on the arm with the paper–a Washington paper, I could tell, because I was standing up by now, right at the front of the gate. But Daddy didn't look at me. He looked at the window washer and winked, so that his tanned face gathered up in a seashell swirl of wrinkles around his eye.

"Risk one eye," I thought. The joke he was always telling about a girl who fell off a balcony during a bone-chilling sermon. She was lucky enough to catch the chandelier, but that left her in a compromising position, and the preacher told the congregation that if they looked up, the Lord would strike them blind. So this one guy in the audience puts a hand over one eye, looks up, and says, "I think I'll risk one eye."

That's what my father taught me about religion: that it was only worth one eye.

But Daddy didn't even risk one eye on me at the airport. Just like no one in that story seemed worried about whether the girl would fall or not, but only whether people would see her underpants. I'm not even sure whether he knew I was there.

The window washer must've been hypnotized by Joan's tiny nipples biting into the smooth surface of her silk dress.

Either that or he was waiting for my father all along. He picked up the bucket of soapy water and moved closer. Daddy dropped something and it plopped into the pail. Warm water splashed onto my bare leg. I was standing that close. And my father didn't even see me–or worse, he saw me and pretended not to. But I was connected to whatever happened because I felt the spill.

I turned around, went back to the parking garage and told Ma'am that he wasn't on the flight.

"I think we'll let him pay for his own taxi," she said. Her checkbook was on the dashboard, and I could see that she'd been figuring out the bills in her head.

"What's Daddy doing in Washington anyway?"

"He's going to topless fund-raisers with Larkin," she said. "He's getting a feel for the pro circuit."

"Really."

"Really. Why are you scratching your leg?"

My skin was still warm where the water splashed me. It felt like a razor burn, where half the skin gets scraped off so there's a shiny white chip in your tan, like a soap scud that didn't get rinsed off in the shower.

"Mosquito bite," I said. "So doesn't he tell you this stuff?"

"Only when he needs advice. I didn't know you were interested in politics."

She pulled out of the parking garage and the car lurched off the curb. I could tell she was going to drive crooked all the way home.

"I'm not," I said. "I just like to know what's going on once in a while." I scraped my leg against the raised metal strip on the car door and hoped she wouldn't notice. "Don't you want to know what's going on?"

"Once in a while. Just like you. Are you going to stop that, or do I have to strap your leg to the seat belt?"

"OK. I stopped. I'm done already. See?" I stretched my leg out in front of me. But there were three red scratches

174

on it, like lashes of cherry licorice, and blood was dripping down the side.

"Libby, my God." She forced the brakes right in the middle of an intersection, and my stomach jumped in two directions.

"Libby, I don't want to see you do that ever again. You've got to stop it. Are you listening to me?"

"What? It doesn't even hurt. Look, Ma'am, the people are starting to get mad back there."

"I don't give a damn if it's the whole blasted electoral college lining up to throw their vote."

Cars were honking in three keys, long and short and interspersed with curses.

"Do you understand what I mean?" she said.

"I'll stop if you stop," I mumbled, underneath my breath.

She jerked forward, and I was afraid she was going to hit me, but she only moved the gearshift into park. She grabbed her purse off the seat between us, pulled out a crumpled tissue, and wiped at my leg, roughly, as if she were trying to rub out a stain. It stung, and there was the smell of nail polish remover everywhere.

"My father's sleeping with someone else," I said, and then she did slap me, and the traffic buzzed and broke and started sweeping by.

I turned my head. Cyril's shadow passed over me, as he paced around the room one more time.

I couldn't see Russ anymore, but I heard him trudging up the stairs. Slowly, favoring his left hip, the way he did when we wrestled, giving me another chance to follow him.

But I was too serious for that by now.

Cyril stopped in front of me and touched my hair. My chin, my cheek, my nose. His hand was chapped and cold, but there was more feeling in it than in my father's or my mother's, who had to pretend the world was satin all the time.

"All alone," he said. "But then, a virgin's always alone. That's what makes her closer to God." He let his hand dangle onto my neck, where he pressed it to my throat and held it over my voice box.

And I was glad, because I was afraid that if he didn't hold me like that, the voice or spirit or demon would burst out of me, it was beating so hard into his hand.

"I've written your name in the palm of my hand," he said, and I remembered the knife there, in my hand, in my pocket.

I slid it out and felt its slick blade against my arm. Then I eased the handle back and sliced in. It was smooth and easy as cutting into a wedding cake. There was no pain. The blood welled out of the cut, letting me see the trail I'd made.

Cyril squatted down beside me to look. Then I did what you would've done a long time before. I grabbed onto the strap of his overalls and cut into Cyril too.

xvi

If you're not a woman, you can forget how thin blood real-ly is. You imagine it pulpy as tomato juice, slow and grainy as a tongue on your thigh. You like to think of it leaving a body with regret, like jellyfish creeping out of the sea. You don't want to watch it dribble out of you with nothing to stop it but your own hands.

Cyril didn't, I could tell.

I cut him in a soft place between his collarbone and the long, flat plate of his left breast muscle. He groaned. The knife stalled against something stringy. I hesitated. Then he grabbed it away from me and threw it onto the floor. He was still squatting in front of me, and I saw that the cut was deeper than I'd thought, the upper edge curled back and purple like the frill of a party favor, or a fish's gill. Below it, blood dripped down in a solid stream, not squirting the way Jesus' wounds did in all the pictures. It was seeping into his overalls, so I couldn't tell how much he'd lost.

I lifted my cut arm to his chest and smeared my blood into his. It was sticky, drying already, and I pressed so hard that the skin squeaked between us. "Fair is fair," I said, even though my stomach was squeezed up in a tight pinecone in my chest.

Then the cut started hurting, as if Cyril's blood were the secret added ingredient that crystallized all my hazy unhappiness into actual pain. I thought of the perfume I rubbed into my paper cut at home, the nail polish remover on Ma'am's crumpled-up tissue. Still, it didn't hurt any more than lying on a hot radiator grate or pressing down into the bedsprings.

He picked me up, rising beneath me like the turtle the

world is supposed to be built on. Then he carried me over to the stained bathtub and set me down inside, where the porcelain was so cold against my bare legs that it made me forget what was happening with my arm. He unhooked his overalls, and I saw that he was streaked with blood all down one side, and that he was naked underneath; the long, soft glut of his stomach ended in a spiky black blossom with three raw pink parasites stirring inside, like newborn baby birds. He wiped at the blood with the overalls, then touched a finger to the cut, shivered, and pulled it away. His standing there reminded me of Joan when she pulled the Band-Aid off her nipple–that same pose, the whole body circled around one breast. Like the piper in the art book Ma'am showed me, holding his pipe away from his mouth, down by his chest, and testing the stops. "That's civilization," she told me, "When they start to show men with musical instruments instead of weapons." But I wasn't sure about civilization, or whether this was all that different.

Cyril tried touching his cut again, and this time he left his hand there longer. My arm surged with an electric pulse. The pain swabbed up and then receded, disappeared. I held onto my elbow and felt its echo. Then Cyril moved his finger all along the knife's track. Down in his body hair, the huddled pink mounds started to move and take shape. His penis eased out over the rest–rubbery and alive, with the smooth cap of a mushroom and a sad, wrinkled stem. Drooping down and down, almost touching the edge of the bathtub. I wanted it to touch. I counted the seconds until it did, my pulse ticking loud, my skin sticking to the porcelain in the cold. But it never happened, because before it could, the whole thing lifted, thickened, and stood up there like a ghost, slanting away from Cyril's body as if it couldn't get straight or lie down, either one. It looked like it hurt, being in two parts that couldn't get together. But Cyril didn't even seem to notice.

"The daughters of men," he said. "And the daughters of men will cut into the sons of God." He wiped the overalls against his crotch, then dropped them on the floor. "It's not beyond Holy Writ. Nothing that I wasn't expecting."

"Samson and Delilah," I said. "Jezebel and Naboth."

"It'll take more than a female to ruin my gospel truth."

I looked at his penis and saw the veins puckered up under skin the color of raw bologna. The pirate's cap folded over and tucked in at the edges. A blind slit at the top, like the opening of a piggy bank.

I wanted to touch him.

But he stopped me and put his hand on my head instead, then pressed it back, so I was looking up at him.

"Libya," he said. "Do you want to serve the Lord or do you want to grow up to be a whore all your life?"

The double pink bag of his scrotum was too close to my face, so close that I could smell its rich stink. The same as dirt smells when something's been buried in it. The hole under the roots of our best mulberry tree where Dot and I put dead birds and bad cooking experiments. The stuff in my stomach divided, split back like the Red Sea.

"It's a basic question. No man can serve two masters. No woman can woo two demiurges."

He let go of my face and now he was swaying again, his penis tilting in front of me. I tried to concentrate on what was underneath. The balls, the jewels, the nuts. All hard words for something so loose and wobbly, a half-empty bag pocked all over with pink goose bumps. Looking like something boiled, something scalded. Holding two uneven lumps, two tough knots caught in the lining of his skin, that you could never take out and look at. Divided and joined, one hanging slightly lower than the other–two valves in a heart.

"The money changers and Pharisees are always calling. The Sadducees are always sodomizing. The prostitutes are always proselytizing. That's where your daddy is now."

Two valves, I thought, one for you and one for me. But neither of them was safe. In or out. Daddy or Cyril. The Lord Jesus or Satan. I couldn't choose.

"But he'll be here soon, the satyred senator. Then we'll see where you put the knife, Libya."

I didn't get to decide. As if I were stuck there inside the bag too, a trick bag, a thick caul where I could suffocate before I ever got myself born.

"Nowhere. Neither," I said. "I'm not playing anymore."

"Too late. As the Lord tells us, it is written."

He pushed my head down into his crotch and held it there like he was dunking or blessing me, or both. His hair scratched against my cheek, smelled of blood and dead leaves and cloves. He put his penis to my lips, so that I could feel its moisture sticking to them, like some sticky sweet liqueur. Then I opened my mouth, he edged it a little farther in, and I could taste its real flavor, almost salty, but more rancid than that–with a harsh astringent tone. Cleaning fluid, I thought. That's what boys are made of.

"There's a mighty enmity between our seed," he said. "He shall bruise thy heel, and thou shalt bruise his head."

He pushed himself in deeper and I almost gagged. Giving head. Making headway. Did it have anything to do with the serpent's head getting bruised? Or was it more my head, the way he fit inside? And when someone didn't want to do it, they said they had a headache.

He pressed into the back of my throat and I got the same panicked sensation as when I used to stand in front of my mirror and try to poke my tonsils with my finger. The feeling of wanting to vomit and then suddenly not, my neck erupting in Christmas tree tinsel running all the way down my arms, which went silky and beautiful as the fur of some exotic animal. I would do it over and over, waiting for the rest of me to be transformed. Into a mermaid. Into a mountain lion. Into a seal. But it seemed as if I'd stay like that, half-alive, half-grown forever. I shifted in the tub and the skin of my knee peeled away from the porcelain. Cyril shivered in my mouth. I got the feeling all the way down to my navel, then below, where it curled around my pelvic bone, metallic and furry at the same time, an impossible troll out of a fairy tale. A troll like Cyril, maybe. I put my arms around his hips, felt the rough putty of his buttocks. I started to help him, opening wider, working the thing around in my mouth. "You can't get over it, you can't get under it, you can't get around it, you must come in at the door," I thought. I came in at the door, and now I was drowning in the ark. But the ark was supposed to keep a person from drowning. And I didn't know when I could've stopped–when I got the note, when I came to the capitol, when I went inside with Cyril and then let Russ go back to Ada's for my father.

"You must come in at the door." I hummed the song, the vibrations setting off reactions in my lips, between my teeth, under my tongue. Bright sparks like the friction between a train and its tracks, like the thin, accurate torch of a glassblower, like the flat glitter in a stained-glass window. As if I were eating a ray of light that kept turning under my teeth.

The blood in Cyril hummed too, the tiny engine of a hummingbird beating against my lips. And for once, his voice was completely still. I pulled harder. I thought this was supposed to be bad for me–disgusting, degrading, gross. But all I felt was power, what my father must feel when the whole legislature stopped reading their papers and bartering over deals and flirting with pages to listen to him speak. It wasn't just having something expensive or being someone important. Power was more a pace, a clock, a rhythm pouncing like a caged lion against the plate glass window of your mind, rebounding and pouncing, so it was hard to keep your head standing straight on top of your neck.

Cyril gripped my hair. Maybe just to hold on, I thought,

but then he pulled me away.

"Enough," he said. "I'm not going to let you steal any sacred fluids. Not this time."

Which time? As if I'd done it before. Or he was talking to someone else. His eyes looked dead from this angle, the opal eyes of trout cooked with their heads on, the same dazed look as the preacher when I caught him staring out at the congregation during the prayer.

"So what are you saving it for?" I asked him.

He pulled my head farther back, refocused his eyes on mine.

I noticed a flaw in one of them. Like the red spot in the yolk of a fertilized chicken egg.

Then I started to giggle. Hard, cold giggles, as if I were coughing up glass. Trying not to, the way Dot and I did when Ma'am had people over and we sat making adult conversation for as long as we could, drinking weak tea out of pearlized coffee cups and kicking each other's bare legs under the dining room table. We held the laughter down in the pits of our stomachs where it grew and changed shape and pressed against our sides. Until we couldn't keep it there anymore, no matter how badly we wanted to, and it bubbled up through our chest cavities, bumping bone, displacing musculature, stretching the range of our windpipes, and we finally felt its ticklish pressure in our throat, tasted its fairy breath filling our mouths with clover and honeysuckle and brownies.

"In the basement," Ma'am would say, pressing her lips together so her pretty face flattened out, bitter dents collapsing all the sweet spots.

Then Dot and I ran down to the laundry room and landed in baskets of dirty clothes, coughing, spitting, gargling, yodeling laughter out as if it came from a bottomless container, the wine vessels at the Wedding at Cana or the oil lamps of the wise virgins. We threw Ma'am's school blouses and Daddy's colored shorts at each other, wrapped our heads in towels, knocked down the ironing board, crawled into the crawl space behind the stairs, lifted our shirts and rubbed each other's sore bellies while we told stories about what we'd do to our company when we grew up and had a house of our own.

And now I was half-grown and I still couldn't stop. "What are you saving it for?" I said. "That's what my boyfriend always says to me when we're playing around in the basement. 'What are you saving it for, Lib, the turn of the century?' And then I laugh at him and he doesn't know why I'm laughing. But maybe he's the one who's saving up, huh? Maybe he's worried about his sacred fluids."

Cyril scrunched down next to the tub and put his face up to mine. "I can say one thing, your pa isn't too worried about it."

I moved away, sat down flat in the bathtub. "So what is it with you two? Are you going to overturn the government or what?"

"Wheel within a deal," Cyril said. "I got the papers for him. We could throw the governor out of office tomorrow, but now the senator's sweet on him again. Seems like your Daddy's just got a sweet tooth."

"What did he do?" I twisted the ragged edge of my dress around my finger. "The governor, I mean."

Cyril stepped over the edge of the bathtub and sat down across from me, his legs mixed up with mine. His penis leaned against his thigh, relaxing into its curve. He ran his fingers over his cut again, scratched his leg, picked up my ankle and squeezed it between his hands, kneading it as if it were a piece of biscuit.

"Contracting bribes. Drug smuggling. Catering to country clubs. Just corruption as usual."

"So why does anybody care?"

"He crossed the wrong lines. He signed that highway art bill just so he could infiltrate the public transportation commission and shortchange the money changers."

"Senator Mills," I said. "Larkin."

He nodded his head.

I put my hand on his ankle too. "Joan's dad. What's he got to do with it?"

"Construction mogul. Building mansions here below."

"Heavenly highways," I said.

"Paved with bad intentions."

"So what's your thing about it?"

He reached up my leg and pulled me toward him, so I was almost sitting in his lap again. "Save the world. Destroy the Antichrist. Undress dignitaries' daughters. Get my name in the papers."

I laughed. "Get cut up in brawls."

He licked his finger and rubbed some of the drying blood off my arm. Rough, chapped, warm—the touch went through me in layers, like the different levels of hot and cold in a lake. Until it got heavy again and sunk past the pit of my stomach, nestled sluglike in my groin.

"Do you really have to save up your sacred fluids to save the world?" I said, then leaned over and licked his chest, tasted the metal in his blood, sharp as blue cheese aged in a cave in a faraway country. Sometimes, the taste rose in my mouth just from having my period. Then I knew it was about to happen. And I'd avoid people—my mother, boys, even Dot—because I was afraid of what I'd do or say.

Cyril shivered again. He put his hands on my breasts like he was trying to get warm. "All the sacred texts recommend it," he said.

My nipples pulled at my chest, thistles in the flesh that were actually part of me. "Let's do it," I said. "Let's do whatever people do."

Cyril raised his eyebrows, first one, then the other. "And we'll call it, what? Rape, sodomy, pederasty, bribery, extortion, abortion?"

"I don't know. We'll think up a name for it later."

"Just in time for the police report," he said, and brushed

my hair away from my neck, started unbuttoning what was left of the neat blue dress I'd put on that morning in my mother's house, when I was a different person.

I watched the dress divide, my grimy white bra open back to front, so the cups eased open with phantom breasts larger than my real ones. "I don't know what to call it," I said, gritting my teeth. "What does my father call it?"

Cyril stretched my arms out and lifted the bra off me, carefully as taking a dress off its hanger. A hanger off its dress. I didn't know which was which anymore, whether my body was the base of things or just the decoration.

"Government," Cyril said. "I think he calls it government."

I stood up, and the rest of my dress slipped off. Then I rolled down my underwear. Against the wall of the ark, my shadow stood tall and flat-chested and childish. My hair was matted up in a kind of ponytail, where Cyril had been holding it. My breasts barely punctured the outline, snow cones in the cold, and my legs wavered, held together like the tail of a mermaid. This was me, I thought, as far away from everybody else as I could get. Nobody's. Not my mother's, not my father's, not Michael's, not even Cyril's—not yet. I held my arms away from my body to get a better look. I wanted to remember. I wanted to know this was me for as long as possible.

Then Cyril pulled me down on top of him and my shadow began to move, my hair falling out of its tangles into a floating crest, my hands gripping the edge of the bathtub and my shoulders hunched over, shivering like wings, like the wings of a trained falcon still clutching the falconer's wrist, but trying all the time to get free.

xvii

Cyril pushed my knees out to either side of him and they ground against the porcelain of the bathtub, cold bone on bone. I thought of reading the letter on my bedroom floor, my knee pressed to my metal bedframe, all my bones connected to that one point of sensation, just so I could finish the note without coming apart, my legs and arms and breasts separating and ganging up on me the way you said they would. I tried to bring my legs closer together, dug them into Cyril's warm sides, till I was sure I must be hurting him, pinning his excess skin to the tub. But I didn't care. The blood on his chest was dried into blobs of raspberry jelly, and he smelled like rare cooked lamb, with spices rising out of him.

He ran his hands over the inside of my thighs, played with the string of the tampon, twisted it against my skin, as if he were loosening the waxy wick of a candle. Then he crooked his finger up into me and rooted out the tampon without even using its string.

Once it was gone, he kept moving his finger around inside, so the blood made a slurping sound. I listened to it until I could predict its pattern, the slick skin ticking beneath me, holding me up above Cyril, up above you all, so I didn't have to act like one of Daddy's people anymore. Slick, what my father called me. That and sly. Slick, sly, the blood said. Slick and sly. Slick and sigh. Skin and sky. The blood tells—my grandmother warned my mother about that. And now my blood was talking to me. From the only place it could get out of. Like all those jokes about chatterboxes. "Cover up your box," my grandfather used to say, when our shorts were too short or he wanted us to be quiet. It didn't matter to him. It was all the same thing. Thinking about it made my nerves curl up toward the spot where my knit summer shorts would cling: my phantom self curled up like a piece of paper—a map—someone had rolled into a tube or telescope so that it would never stay flat again.

You did that too. When I thought you wouldn't. You rolled me into a telescope so you could look at my father. You pressed me flat to the car door in the parking garage, to the dirt road, to the bedsprings, and tried to make a map out of me. The same as the map we read in the car, dividing up the population of Danitria, Kimball, North Fork. So we'd know what kind of split to expect there. You just wanted to know the kind of split we'd make, the grain of the wood, the set of the wishbone. A split of loyalties, capital gains, champagne.

Split.

Split, sly, the blood said.

Some kind of a joke, I thought.

Cyril was talking now too. "And you shall know the truth," he said. "And the truth shall make you heave."

"What truth? Like about the letter?"

"About this," he said, "Right about here," and he pulled my torso down over his penis, lifted its cap to the opening in me.

I knew how it was supposed to go, but I didn't believe it could happen. A ship in a bottle. Sex is a ship in a bottle, I thought. Only in this case, it's an ark. It would be like having the whole ark inside of me. Like eating the world.

He had the tip in, and that didn't really hurt. Just the nose of an animal exploring.

"Tell me how much you want. How much truth can you take, Libya?"

He pushed in farther, and now it did hurt. I thought of Joan and the broken glass, the neck of the bottle exploding.

"You move, Sibyl. It's better if you break your own seals

instead of waiting for old Satan to do it."

"I can't," I said. "I can't move. I'm afraid my insides will come out."

He put his sticky hand around my waist, tipped me toward him, nuzzled my sore breast. "The temple veil tore from the top to the bottom. That's what made it miraculous. That's why you're tearing from the top."

I tried to imagine the curtain in the holy of holies, but I only came up with the dingy dust ruffle hanging from my bed at home. Ripped from the top or bottom, what did it matter? It wasn't going to last me until I went to college anyway. But then, I didn't want to linger around like that, waiting for people to disappoint me so much I didn't have anything left to tear into. What's a dust ruffle for, after all? Just so no one can see what you've got stuffed under your bed? On the day I got the letter I had two packages of clove cigarettes, the bra I was wearing the first time I kissed Michael, a soap dish Dot and I pickpocketed from the bathroom at Daddy's club, my old retainer, and a dirty book about ski instructors in the clean blue Alps that I bought on sale at the mall and read over and over when I was feeling disgusted. The only things in the world that my mother didn't know about me. And even those were prettied up and pitiful, hiding behind a lacy red-and-white screen, like some dumb puppet-show of being a teenager. I could never keep up with my father, in that department. I could never keep up with my father at all.

I felt a cramp shoot up in me, though no one had moved. My insides creaked, they were clinging so close together, peach halves canned in their own syrup or fat pigeons huddling in a cage. I contracted around Cyril. Tight. Contracted. Like a deal. A contract and a contradiction. That's what it was between us, just a contraction. Not that I loved him or hated him or wanted him or not. Only that we were contracted together, working on the same deal.

He settled me onto his penis, hooked me into his story,

like all those stick figures connected by penises on the outside of the boat. Now something's happening to me, I thought, when I was afraid it never would. Now I'm breaking outside the fence they talk about at church, where jumping over just one fencepost, landing on just one penis, sets you outside the law and the Lord's pasture for good.

Outside your church.

Outside your family.

Outside the story everyone has planned for you, the one where you go to college and marry and become a woman as unhappy as your mother scrubbing the bathtub in a slip.

I started to move. And I laughed, no matter how much it hurt, because I was in a bathtub now, maybe part of her story after all. I pushed down onto Cyril until I felt my pelvic bone touch his. The cramp turned into a sharper trill, vibrating in my backbone, in the cavities of my teeth. Something wet–blood?–touched my pubic hair, where it gristled against his. He pulled my hands off the bathtub and put them on his shoulders, close to his neck, as if I were choking him. Then he lifted me up by the waist, squeezing all his energy into me, waited for a beat, and dropped me back down on top of him. The ring of my vagina burned, and my singed finger surged in sympathy. He lifted me again, like in the hymn, where Jesus promises he'll lift you up if you're just willing to stay put long enough.

I didn't think I could stay put. And that was why I started helping, because it seemed to hurt less that way. Not because it actually felt good, at least not at first. I just knew I had to do it to get to the outside.

In the end, you always have to rape yourself, is what I learned from you.

So I moved down and up again, creaking and dizzy, like a horse on a merry-go-round.

His face broke into wrinkles, cracked sidewalks spreading out from his eyes. I couldn't tell which of us was in pain anymore. "Jezebel," he said. "Mary Deborah Jael Ruth."

190

I moved again. "I'm here," I said. And I really thought I was.

But now it seemed like I was hurting him, stabbing, stubbing, stumping along. For my mother and my father and Ada and the way the whole world seemed to count on me staying still, staying innocent, staying dead so I could stay alive. I pumped harder, as if I were riding on the pommel of a saddle. The smell of blood, spice, and dirt got closer around us, like we were wrapped in an unwashed blanket of ourselves. And bucking to get out. Blood in a bathtub. I remembered the time I threw my leg over my bicycle and cut my toes on a broken panel of glass leaning against the garage wall. I hopped all the way up the stairs on one foot, thinking I'd stubbed my toe. But I must've known, really, because I went straight for the bathtub, and when I looked down, the blood was already puddling between the ridges of the bath mat. I pulled it up and threw it out onto the floor, as if its sea anemone spikes were what was making me bleed, then screamed for Dot, who was beading necklaces on the floor of our parents' bedroom. She came in with the needle still in her hand, a tail of blue and yellow beads hanging from it.

"Ommm," she said. "I bet you're gonnna have to get stitches."

Ma'am and Daddy were gone, at some Sunday afternoon tea, and for a minute, I thought Dot was going to take her beads and needle and stitch me up herself.

"I'm serious," I said. "I'm seriously dying."

"Just stop it," she told me. "Hold your horses. Hold your toes together, and I'll run over and get them."

But I didn't. Instead, I leaned over and lifted up the bath mat, squeezed it tight against my arm. On the eggshell tile, the floor was printed with a grid of blood, like the blurry purple ditto worksheets at school. They came off the teacher's desk still wet, smelling of ink, and clinging together like layers of lasagna noodles. I held them up to my nose, draped them, cold and heavy, over my arm, so that when I finally went to read them I could hardly make out the letters.

My foot alternated between numbness and pain. It was funny, it didn't hurt much more than stubbing my toe. Except my heart was beating there like it had slipped down my leg and was panicking to get back up under the ribcage. And I was glad that I'd cut myself when my parents weren't home and probably stained that stupid bathtub my mother was always scrubbing.

I looked at the tile again, where the blood started to seem like a map, or writing. The ridges of the bath mat had made hooks and eyes, *j*s and *o*s and *h*s. The story moved, just maybe an inch, and I thought I could see my future in it, the way they do with tea leaves. There was a single note of static in my ear, and then a whole chord came out of it, so that I could taste each note green and blue and yellow on my tongue, but still knew the flavor they made altogether. The writing split apart too, as if it were trying to make the same harmony.

Then my mother walked into the bathroom.

"Libby," she said. "Baby, what did you do?" Her cold, smooth face was against mine and her hand was reaching for my foot. "Don't worry, love. It's going to be all right. We'll get you to the doctor right away." Her lilac perfume stung my nose like the sharpest sound a pitch pipe could make, and I started to cry, my face wet and melting under her cold cheek.

I was relieved, it's true, but once I started to feel sorry for myself, I knew I wouldn't be able to see anything more. And I always blamed her for that.

But this time, I wasn't going to stop before I got to the finish. I gripped Cyril's collarbone and bore down. He said a name I didn't know, or maybe it wasn't a word at all, just some garbled shout. I heard my teeth grind together, but I didn't feel them touch. Gnashing of teeth, or just my father chewing ice cubes. I thought of Ma'am throwing Daddy's golf shoes into the filled hotel bathtub. And some other story she told me, what was it? A man writing in a bathtub. A man with a disease that made him have to soak in the tub all day while he wrote important letters and documents, sitting there with a board over his lap. There was a famous painting of him; he was lying in the bathtub dead, after someone–a woman–killed him. Because she didn't agree with his politics, Ma'am said. She always laughed about that.

Cyril started moving faster; I had to change my pace to keep up with him. And then the pain started to twist and tweeze into pleasure, copper burnished against copper until it shone, bright pennies of it behind my knees, in the indentations at the tops of my thighs, between the spaces of my backbone. My nipples were foreign coins with strange symbols, veins I'd never known about, heads of princes and queens, mottoes in Greek and Persian, whole histories of the world, stretched out and expanding so far I thought the skin would split.

Split, Sly, the blood said.

Cyril made a gargling sound in his throat. He turned his head and bit my wrist, where I was holding onto him. Then I went numb from that spot on down, so that I couldn't help him move anymore, and he was bucking alone. But the venom, or pleasure, or sin kept sweeping around in me, like the snowstorm picture in the capitol. And I was looking for someone to lead me out. A yellow light, egg yolk broken into a mound of granulated sugar, nutmeg, eggnog, snow ice cream, a pale hand on a lantern, your cold hand holding a light, so that your bones shone through and I could see the note between your fingers and the backward letters on the other side.

A girl who'd rape herself just to get free, then talk about it whether people wanted to hear or not. A man who couldn't decide how much he wanted to succeed. A daughter sacrificed in a boat on a windless sea of prairie. Her mother waiting at home. Scrubbing the bathtub, just in case.

Cyril gripped me and shouted "Jehovah." He couldn't stop anymore, I could tell, it was like pumping a swing so hard you couldn't get your legs to slow down. "Yahweh," he said. "Jehovah God."

Then the swinging stalled, and he wavered a little, lifted me up off him, while I was still spinning in the storm.

I landed next to him, my legs mixed up with his, my back sweating against the cold of the tub. I looked over and saw that his whole lap was filled with blood, matted in his pubic hair and coating his penis so that it looked like a piece of his intestines sticking out.

Or a part of me, an abortion, like he said.

Cyril closed his eyes, and I dipped my finger in the blood, made an X over his eyelid. My legs were shaking, and he put a hand on my thigh.

"Peace, be still," he said. "It only took the Lord six days to create the heavens and the earth. But it took him six millennia to destroy it. And then he really had to rest."

"When did that happen? Did I miss something?" My voice was too high, too fast, too grainy. It sounded younger than I was by now, stuck to the roof of my mouth and the inside of my lips like a sticky sweet liqueur.

"It's always happening, Libya. Whenever there's one of you around. As long as there's even one left."

I put my hand between my legs, to make sure everything was all right, the wobbly folds of doughy skin and the plump raisin between them, sticky with blood but brimming anyway, buzzing with travel, the way they would if I were sitting in the back of a school bus holding a science project in my lap.

I pinched myself together, and decided to ask.

"Is that why you want to cut everybody up? Just because you're trying to get closer to the apocalypse?"

Cyril laughed. His eyes flickered open and his one cheek

puckered, half a dimple, half a scar. "You're the one cutting up, Sibyl. I'm only trying to purge the fold."

He closed his eyes again and I stood up, got dizzy, and caught myself before I fell. The room was darker than it had been before. I walked over to the bug light and sat down, started throwing handfuls of sawdust into the lantern, listening to it sizzle and explode. I could probably go back now if I wanted; Cyril didn't look like he was going to stop me. But I didn't seem to want to go. I picked my leg up and looked for bruises, searched the surface of my breast to find the teeth marks in a perforated halo around the nipple, wondered if Ma'am would take me back, or if it would be like a mother bird rejecting her young after they'd been touched by human hands. Maybe I'd have to move out to Danitria and live with Ada, in Daddy's other family, and make friends with Russ. I shivered. Maybe I'd have to leave the state.

I threw more sawdust into the fire and the sizzling buckled into another sound, bumps and whispers, steps on the stairs.

I could've moved, gotten dressed, woken Cyril, but I just sat still, waiting to see what would happen next.

Daddy walked in first, his jacket still crisp, his blond curls pressed flat on one side. He saw me, and his eyes jarred, flared, and retreated, flat and blue and bitter as pilot lights on an old gas stove. He patted his jacket. Looking for the lighter I'd stolen, I thought, but then he came out with a gun instead. The gun he showed me how to shoot. He held it crooked, like he was trying to aim a shotgun, and Joan walked up behind him and put her hand on his elbow. He shrugged her off and nodded toward me.

Cyril stepped out of the bathtub. I remembered how Daddy couldn't even look at blood. But he stood there without turning away. And I was jealous, because maybe, in my whole life, he'd never stared at me that long.

"Whitehead, good buddy, I just want you to know this

doesn't have anything to do with politics. This is a crime of passion," he said. "You can tell by the whites of my eyes."

Cyril only began to sway. When he started, he was saying words like "Pharisee," "sodomy," "pollution," but then he went into a higher gear, so the sounds all spun together and it was like a whole crowd of people talking at once. A multitude. A cocktail party. A mob. I never knew what they meant by speaking in tongues before. But Cyril was one long red tongue, rolled in red clay, eating dust for all the days of its life, collecting more voices as it went on.

A butterfly vibrated in my voice box, and I wanted to speak too. To tell my father what had happened to me. Cyril. Relic. Lyric. Cyrillic. Whatever was written on the bathmat in blood. Whatever your letter didn't say. There was so much in my mouth that my tongue got in the way, lying there like a slab of fatty meat I couldn't spit up or swallow, no matter how I tried.

That's when I felt a hand on my breast and heard the gun go off.

Cyril spilled over so close to my father that Daddy's coat was spotted with blood and I was afraid he'd shot himself. He leaned over the naked body, spit into a triangular patch of hair low on its back, then lifted the gun and shot again.

Joan's hand made the same motion on my breast, lifting up the lobe, pulling at the nipple. She was so close I smelled her sweat, like balsamic vinegar over the dusky gunpowder, and I knew that she was bleeding too.

"Joan, call the governor," Daddy said. "Call my lawyer. Call the papers."

She smiled. "And what should I tell them?" she asked, pinching me again, so that my nerves vibrated in a filigree of metal filings dancing over a magnet, froze, and dug deeper in the skin, implanted splinters of the story we'd never tell, even when they gave me the morning-after pill and sent me to prep school, Daddy lost his election over the scandal, Ma'am changed her religion and started selling real estate, Joan grew up and became a district court judge.

"Break a few rules," my father said. "Tell them the truth." His eyes curdled, then his face, and he handed her the gun, like he expected her to know what to do with it. "But first clean her up and bring her back down to the house. All right, Libby? 10-4, Sly?"

I didn't say anything, and he left anyway.

Then we were alone with Cyril. She walked over to him, bent down swaying in her high heels, set the gun on the floor and felt his heart, his wrists, the pulse points behind his ears. She pulled a package out of her purse, flexed off the rubber band in a single motion, and dropped the cache of papers onto his back. Letters on yellow legal paper, onionskin, blue-lined stationery, graph sheets, cocktail napkins spilled over the body. I picked one up.

It was greasy on my fingers, as if it had been fingered by many hands.

Dear Libby, it said.

I thought I recognized the print. "Look, it's not even his handwriting. He didn't even know about it, I bet."

She turned, reached behind her shoulder and untwined her jacket. "Libby, honey, he might as well. He would've if someone else hadn't gotten to it first. You know these guys. They're so incompetent that you've just got to hurry them along. Otherwise, they'd be drinking and moaning and preaching over every little thing for decades. I can't wait. I just can't wait anymore, can you?"

"Then where'd they come from?" I said.

"In the mail. I've been collecting them."

I checked her face to see whether she was bluffing and it was bright with sweat caught in her eyebrows, in the blond down over her lip.

"But if they're for me, then why didn't I get to see them before?"

"Don't blame me, I'm just the secretary," she said, and

handed me her jacket. "Anyway, I think you already know what they say."

As she worked my arms into the sleeves, I tried not to look at Cyril's body humped over by the bathtub, stiller than I'd ever seen it, the long back unmarked, its slope articulated like a bridge. Then all she did was touch me and he was back there in my body, tangled in the veins, riding the closed fist of my uterus, climbing the skinny trunks of the fallopian tubes, and I was finally coming out of the snowstorm, coming in circles spreading out, in radio waves, coming around the dizzy curves of the parking garage, back through the turn signals on the way home from the club, the secret bends into vacant lots, the crooked hill our house was set into, Ma'am's thin, beautiful mouth that always looked like she was holding pins in it, just about to sew something up. I came over and over, like I was vomiting, and couldn't stop. I couldn't pretend it was finished; I couldn't believe what was about to begin.

The police filed the letters. No one went to jail. No one doubted our word. At the station, I flirted with the young police officer behind the camera as he tried to get just one shot of me looking serious and I laughed through three rounds of film. I didn't recognize the girl in the photo strips he slipped into my hand: scratched, bloody, beautiful, her features bubbling over the edges of her profile and repeated off the frame. I readjusted Joan's jacket around my shoulders; I rubbed at the whisker burn on my neck, clutched the slick filmstrips so hard they pressed their imprint into my palm.

But then, I still feel your mark wherever my skin meets paper. And I can't stay dead any longer, can't stop myself, can't keep quiet, can't give it any rest, and I'm coming for you.